By royal decree, Harlequin Presents is delighted to bring you THE ROYAL HOUSE OF NIROLI. Step into the glamorous, enticing world of the Nirolian Royal Family. As the king ails he must find an heir...each month an exciting new installment follows the epic search for the true Nirolian king. Eight heirs, eight romances, eight fantastic stories! Favorite author Penny Jordan starts this fabulous new series with *The Future King's Pregnant Mistress*. It's time for playboy Prince Marco Fierezza to claim his rightful place—on the throne! But what will the king-in-waiting do when he discovers his mistress is pregnant?

Plus, Lucy Monroe brings you the final part of her MEDITERRANEAN BRIDES duet, *Taken: The Spaniard's Virgin,* where Miguel takes Amber's innocence.There's another sexy Spaniard in Trish Morey's *The Spaniard's Blackmailed Bride,* when Blair is blackmailed into marriage but Diablo's touch sets her body on fire! In *Bought for the Greek's Bed* by Julia James, Theo demands his new bride also be his wife in the bedroom. In *The Greek Millionaire's Mistress* by Catherine Spencer, Gina Hudson goes to settle an old score in Athens, only to fall into the arms—and bed!—of a tycoon. *The Sicilian's Red-Hot Revenge* by Kate Walker has a handsome, fiery Italian who wants revenge, but what happens when he discovers he's going to be a father? In Annie West's *The Sheikh's Ransomed Bride,* powerful Sheikh Rafiq rescues Belle from rebels, only to demand marriage in return! And in Maggie Cox's *The Millionaire Boss's Baby,* a brooding boss's sensual seduction proves too good to resist. Enjoy!

Chosen by him for business,
taken by him for pleasure...

A classic collection of office romances from Harlequin Presents by your favorite authors

Look out for more, coming soon!

Maggie Cox

THE MILLIONAIRE BOSS'S BABY

IN Bed WITH THE Boss

TORONTO • NEW YORK • LONDON
AMSTERDAM • PARIS • SYDNEY • HAMBURG
STOCKHOLM • ATHENS • TOKYO • MILAN • MADRID
PRAGUE • WARSAW • BUDAPEST • AUCKLAND

ISBN-13: 978-0-373-12650-7
ISBN-10: 0-373-12650-6

THE MILLIONAIRE BOSS'S BABY

First North American Publication 2007.

This edition published by arrangement with Harlequin Books S.A.

www.eHarlequin.com

Printed in U.S.A.

All about the author...
Maggie Cox

MAGGIE COX loved to write almost as soon as she learned to read. Her favorite occupation was daydreaming and making up stories in her head; this particular pastime has stayed with her through all the years of growing up, starting work, marrying and raising a family. No matter what was going on in her life, whether joy, happiness, struggle or disappointment, she'd go to bed each night and lose herself in her imagination.

For many years she secretly filled exercise books and then her word processor with her writing, never showing anyone what she wrote. It wasn't until she met her second husband, the love of her life, that she was persuaded to start sharing those stories with a publisher. Maggie settled on Harlequin as she has loved reading romance novels since she was a teenager. After several rejections, the letters that were sent back from the publisher started to become more and more positive and encouraging, and in July 2002 she sold her first book.

The fact that she is being published is truly a dream come true, however each book she writes is still a journey in "courage and hope" and a quest to learn and grow and be "the best writer she can." Her advice to aspiring authors is "Don't give up at the first hurdle, or even the second, third or fourth, but keep on keeping on until your dream is realized. Because if you are truly passionate about writing and learning the craft, as Paulo Coelho states in his book *The Alchemist,* 'The Universe will conspire to help you make it a reality.'"

To Evelyn, John and Stephen with all my love

CHAPTER ONE

IT HAD been a long, seemingly endless journey—the most ambitious drive Georgia had undertaken in ages. Her saving grace was that she adored driving and prided herself at being quite good at it. With her Labrador Hamish in the back behind her she had the best companion she could wish for, next to her brother Noah. Now, well into the summer evening, she drove silently, with the radio off, her gaze lapping up the extraordinarily beautiful landscape of the Scottish Glens, tiredness banished by what had to be one of the most heavenly sights on earth.

Everywhere she looked she was treated to the most incredible beauty—sunlit lochs, mountain peaks and shimmering green fields. Even Hamish seemed to perk up as he looked out of the window, as if silently contemplating the large open spaces in which to romp and run free with eager relish. It was a far cry from the overcrowded London suburb where Georgia lived.

Already she sensed the accumulated knots and kinks of tension in her back start to unravel a little.

They had made quite a few stops during the long journey, for food and drink, but they had still made very good time. Now, Georgia knew, by the map opened on the seat beside her, as well as her new boss's very precise e-mail directions, that there was not too much further to go before they reached Glenteign—the large country estate of which he was Laird.

'No wonder Noah loved working here!' she declared out loud, and Hamish wagged his tail enthusiastically as if to agree.

Her brother had assured her that she would grow to love Glenteign too. He'd recently spent six months there, in his capacity as a freelance garden designer hired to help work on the formal gardens. It was a place where a person could really *breathe,* he'd told her, his passion for nature and beauty spilling over into his voice. And in his opinion Georgia wouldn't regret leaving London behind for a while, with its continual gridlocked traffic and polluted air. Working as the Laird's temporary secretary, while his permanent secretary recovered from a bad fall, she would have some breathing space from the grinding commute into the City every day. She would find out what a different way of life it was up here—a much more relaxed, 'sane' way of life.

She had accepted the job because she wanted so much to believe him, but Georgia still had some reservations about her decision. What would it be like working for a man who had probably never had to worry about where the next meal was coming from in his life? A man who, because of his status, epitomised the old feudal system of 'Lord of the Manor' while those around him were mere serfs?

She didn't exactly have a problem with the concept of inherited wealth—she begrudged nobody their comfortable circumstances—it was just that she was so weary sometimes of her own struggle to keep the wolf from the door, and the idea that somebody could just be born into such good fortune and not have to do anything to earn it was apt to rub salt into the wound. Still, no doubt the wealthy Laird of Glenteign had his own problems…they just didn't come in the same shape as Georgia's. But—problems or no—surely he couldn't fail to take solace in so much wonderful scenery?

When her reliable but old Renault finally drew into the grounds of Glenteign, Georgia switched off the engine, leaned her elbow on the window's ledge and considered her surroundings with a flare of wonderment in the pit of her stomach.

The house immediately proclaimed its historic past—its impressive edifice of Pictish stone, with its turrets reaching towards the presently cloudless azure sky, reminding Georgia of an ancient impenetrable fortress that had survived every onslaught both nature and man could throw at it and still there it stood, proud and inviolable, with an almost defiant grace. Turning her head, Georgia viewed the lushness of emerald lawns rolling out into the distance like an expansive glittering carpet, and over to the right a high stone wall that perhaps led to the formal gardens that her brother had been working on for the past half-year.

She couldn't deny she was eager to see them—not just because of the work Noah had done there, but because he'd told her they were incredibly beautiful. Moving her gaze further afield, a grove of tall firs captured her attention, stretching endlessly beyond the exquisite perfection of the immaculate lawns. There was just so much land! It didn't seem feasible that one person could own all of this. She began to realise what a prestigious opportunity this was for Noah, coming to work here. And now, because of the success he had achieved, he was working at another large estate in the Highlands—a commission he had secured on the Laird's recommendation because he had been so impressed with what he'd done at Glenteign.

She felt a flicker of love and pride. Every sacrifice she'd made to help Noah get his business off the ground had been worth it…

'You found us, then?'

Abruptly lured away from her reverie, Georgia found her glance commanded by a pair of eyes that were so faultlessly, intensely blue that for a moment no speech was possible on her part. The rest of the features in the masculine face before here were not exactly difficult to look at either. It was as if they might have been sculpted—the planes and angles so strongly delineated that they were surely the loving work of an artist's reverent hand? But Georgia wasn't the only one who was transfixed… The man's unflinching perusal of her own face came as a shock.

She wasn't used to being regarded with such uncommon directness and everything inside her clenched hard in sudden self-consciousness. But before she could find her voice, he was opening the driver's door and standing aside for her to step out onto the gravel.

'Yes…hello.' She held out her hand, then awkwardly withdrew it almost as soon as her skin came into contact with his. *Such an acceptably polite gesture shouldn't feel as if it was bordering on intimacy but somehow it did.* As he considered her further, his gaze no less direct, Georgia silently bemoaned her travel-worn appearance. After several hours' travelling her clothes must resemble unironed laundry, she was sure. The cream linen shift dress she wore, with its scooped neckline, had been cool and fresh when she'd donned it early this morning, but it definitely didn't look like that now.

'Did you have a good journey?'

Beneath the polite questioning Georgia thought she detected a slight strain—as though he neither welcomed nor enjoyed this kind of inconsequential chit-chat. Her heart sank a little.

'Yes, I did. The directions you gave me were spot-on.'

'Good.'

'I presume you must be the Laird?'

'Yes, I am… And you are Georgia…Noah's sister.'

It was a statement of fact, not requiring a reply.

'How do I address you?' she asked, her voice determinedly bright.

'The correct title is "Chief," but I would be quite happy for you to call me Keir—the same as I told your brother. Talking of which…I have to say I can hardly see a resemblance between the two of you.'

'People usually say that.'

'Then I'm sorry to be so predictable.'

He was still a little perturbed by the handshake they'd shared—although the contact had been less than brief, Keir had been genuinely taken aback by the warm electrical 'buzz' that had flowed straight through him. It had been a very arresting wake-up call, and now he sensed his attention magnetised by

Georgia Cameron's lovely face. He was surprised that she was so different in colouring from her tall, blond, blue-eyed brother, and perhaps more pleased than he should be by the contrast. Anybody with a penchant for beauty would admire such dazzling green-gold eyes, but in a face as animated and compelling as hers, with its high, elegant cheekbones and wide, generous mouth, it was hard not to elevate them as perhaps the most beautiful he'd ever seen…

But Keir could hardly attest to welcoming such distracting assets. It was her professional skills he was interested in, not her looks. He had employed her because her brother had assured him that if he was looking for a first-class secretary, he should look no further than his very capable sister. He'd said she was temping with an agency in the City, and her current job would be coming to an end soon, so she could start at Glenteign practically straight away.

Way behind with the administration of running such a large estate, after reluctantly inheriting the mantle of Laird from his brother Robert, who'd been killed in an accident abroad, Keir was in urgent need of some first class secretarial and organisational skills. Doubly so since his own secretary Valerie had unfortunately tumbled down the stairs and broken her leg. *Only the next few days would tell if Noah Cameron had exaggerated his sister's capabilities or not…*

'I expect you'd like to go straight to your room and freshen up?'

'There's something that I really need to do first if you don't mind?'

'What's that?'

'I need to take Hamish for a bit of a walk. The poor creature's been cooped up for too long in my small car, and to tell you the truth I feel the same. We won't be ages…is that all right?'

'That's fine. I should have thought of it myself.'

Keir moved to the passenger door behind the driver's seat of Georgia's dusty little car, pulled it open and invited Hamish to jump out. The Labrador was ridiculously grateful, leaping up at him excitedly and wagging his tail at a rate of knots.

'Oh, my gosh—he's taken to you straight away! He doesn't do that with everybody…he must sense that you're friendly.'

Georgia's smile was genuinely delighted.

Being the unexpected recipient of such a fulsome expression of joy, Keir stared—caught between wanting to arouse more of the same rather beguiling delight and needing to assert some formality between them pretty quickly. The truth was he suddenly found himself having serious reservations about the wisdom of employing this rather disarming woman to work for him…even though the post was only temporary.

He decided to try and keep her gestures of friendliness at bay as much as possible. Theirs was a strictly business relationship, and if she didn't come up to scratch then Keir would have no compunction in telling her she was no longer needed. And he wouldn't cut her any slack just because her brother had impressed him either. James Strachan certainly wouldn't have. A less compassionate and sentimental man would have been hard to find anywhere! And, even though his father had shown evidence of relenting his rather austere manner towards the end of his life, the die had been cast. His efforts to try and forge with his younger son an emotional bond that had never existed before had come too late, Keir acknowledged with some bitterness. It had certainly come too late for his brother Robbie…

'I wouldn't read too much into it,' Keir said, deliberately pushing his hands into the pockets of his light coloured chinos, as if signalling that he wouldn't be paying the animal any undue attention while he was there. He had agreed to her request to bring the dog with her, and that should be enough. 'He's just grateful to be let out. You can walk anywhere, but I'd be glad if you kept the dog away from the flowerbeds. Is your stuff in the boot? All the staff in the house are busy, so I'll take it upstairs to your room. It's on the second floor. I'll leave the door open so that you know which one it is. Dinner is at eight, and I like people to be prompt. Enjoy your walk.'

Her smile gone, Georgia frowned and murmured, 'Thanks.' And if the withdrawal of that smile made Keir feel as if he'd deliberately deprived himself of something extraordinary, then he told himself he deserved it. Watching her collect Hamish's lead from her handbag beside the driver's seat and walk away, he opened the car boot and lifted out her luggage to carry it into the house.

Freshly showered after her walk round the grounds with Hamish, Georgia sat on the bed in her room and examined the employment contract Keir had left for her to sign. *He didn't waste much time, did he?* What did he think she was going to do? Run away after driving since the early hours of the morning to get here?

Even though she might have briefly entertained the thought, after the distinctly frosty way he'd shut down on her following her remark about Hamish liking him, Georgia was not about to give him the satisfaction. She would show Keir Strachan, Laird of Glenteign, that she was a reliable, efficient and skilled worker—and most of all that she kept her word when a promise was made.

Signing her name with a deliberate flourish, she laid the paperwork aside, then shook her damp hair free from the towel she'd wrapped it in. Pushing her fingers through the dark slippery strands, she let her gaze wander over her new surroundings. The room was the height of elegance, with plenty of loving feminine touches everywhere—from the rose-pink velvet curtains, with their matching gathered tie-backs and deep swags, to the rather grand mahogany dressing table with its gleaming surfaces, ornate lace doilies and sparkling oval-shaped mirror. The drowsy scent of late summer pervaded the air, and there was a breathtaking bouquet of white roses in a pink vase arranged on top of a polished satinwood chiffonier that made Georgia's heart skip with pleasure.

She wondered who had been responsible for such a delightful touch. Noah had told her that Keir wasn't married, so it must be some other female… Georgia felt vaguely annoyed that she was even speculating about it at all. She should be concentrating on getting ready to present herself to her new boss; that was what she should be doing!

Jumping up, she went to fetch her hairdryer from her almost empty suitcase. Realising that it was almost ten to eight, an unwelcome twist of anxiety knotted her stomach at the recollection that her new employer expected people to be 'prompt' for dinner. Trying to quell the feeling of rebellion that the thought surprisingly inspired, she turned her mind instead to the prospect of meeting the other staff who worked in the house.

Noah had told her how fond he'd grown of Keir's housekeeper, Moira Guthrie, while he'd worked there, and if the woman was as friendly as he had described then perhaps she needn't be as daunted as she was feeling at present at the idea of living in such a grand, impressive residence. Not to mention acting as secretary to a man who appeared to welcome gestures of friendliness with about as much enthusiasm as finding a viper in his bed!

Unlike her bedroom, the dining room had plenty of masculine touches in evidence—from the array of shining swords placed strategically round the walls to the several portraits of presumably past lairds who overlooked the proceedings with a definitely superior air. Breathtakingly impressive, the room was decorated in true baronial splendour. In fact, as she'd followed the very amiable Moira Guthrie inside, Georgia had half expected a fanfare to sound.

She bit down on her lip to suppress a smile. Under its high-raftered ceilings and candle sconces on the walls, and seated at the long refectory table with its burnished silverware and elegant cream dinner service, it was easy to imagine herself transported to a much more elegant and mannered era. All this finery was a far cry from Georgia and Noah's ridiculously small dining room at home, with its well-used pine table bought at a local second-hand store, and the four matching chairs that were in urgent need of refurbishment…

Glancing briefly down at her simple pink cotton dress, worn with the heart-shaped rose quartz pendant that her mother had left her, Georgia couldn't help musing that her employer might expect much more elegant attire in her dressing for dinner in his imposing house. Oh, well… Noah hadn't seemed to worry about such things, and nor should she. Neither of them had ever been able to afford elegant clothes even if they'd desired them. Most of the time they had been too busy just trying to survive.

Bereft of both parents since Noah was fourteen, Georgia, just five years his senior, had taken over her brother's care from that too young age, and worrying about finances had dominated her life for more years than she cared to remember. Even to the point of sacrificing any opportunity for a loving relationship, according to her concerned friends. But there was no real sacrifice in Georgia's mind. She would do it all again tomorrow if she had to. Still, she couldn't deny that the valuable commission to help work on the gardens at Glenteign had literally arrived in the nick of time.

Georgia had sunk every spare penny she'd had after paying the bills and running their home into

Noah's fledgling gardening business. With her blessing, he was intending to reinvest as much of the cash he'd received from that commission into making the business even more viable… In a couple of years' time maybe they would both be able to relax a little where money was concerned, instead of working practically every hour God sent.

'Don't worry, my dear…we won't be so formal every night,' Moira assured Georgia, having seen the doubt flicker across her face. 'We do like to do things properly at the weekends, but during the week we're very informal. There's a smaller dining room, just down the hall from the kitchen, and we usually eat in there. Now, if you'll excuse me for a second, I'm just off to see where Chief Strachan is. I expect he's busy finishing off some work and has forgotten the time. God knows the poor man's been up to his eyes in it since he came back here! And what with poor Valerie breaking her leg, you haven't arrived a moment too soon, lassie, and that's a fact!'

Georgia breathed a sigh of relief when the other woman exited the room. She couldn't deny she welcomed a few moments by herself, to reflect on where she'd landed. Considering the job in hand, there was no doubt in her mind about her secretarial abilities passing muster—but, having finally met her new boss, she did have some concerns as to whether they would get along. Lord knew, it could be frankly exhausting working for someone without a sense of humour, and quite honestly Georgia had been hoping for a breakthrough in that department. People in London these days seemed so uptight, with most of them consumed by long working hours and making career goals their God, that it made working as a temporary secretary for such driven individuals sometimes frankly hellish.

Sighing, she got up from her chair to examine the paintings that bedecked the walls. Turning up her nose at the stern male portraits to rest her gaze instead on the more genial scenes of pastoral serenity that were so invitingly displayed alongside them, she felt a little of the anxiety she was holding in her body ease from her shoulders.

'My apologies for keeping you waiting.'

She turned at the sound of that richly attractive and commanding voice, her gaze diverted by the sight of Keir walking straight to the head of the table in a brisk manner, straightening the cuffs on his open-necked white shirt, as though about to head up a board meeting instead of sitting down to dinner. Surprisingly, he was wearing denim jeans, and the faint aura of some classic male cologne lingered in the air as he moved.

Catching the briefly intense flare of the searching azure glance that immediately came her way, Georgia felt her stomach react as if she'd just plummeted several thousand feet without a parachute. Noah should have warned her that the Laird was so…so compelling! But perhaps it was understandable that younger brothers left out such important details when describing another man to their sisters!

Feeling ridiculously annoyed that she should be so thrown off-centre by her employer's good-looks, when she wasn't remotely an easily impressed girl at all, Georgia lightly shrugged her shoulders.

'Not at all. I was just enjoying looking at your beautiful paintings. The portraits are a little too severe for my taste, if you don't mind my saying…but the country scenes are lovely.'

'You like art?'

'Of course.'

The surprise on her face held the unspoken question. *Doesn't everybody?* and Keir found himself inordinately pleased by her vehemence.

'There are many paintings in the house—some by some very famous Scottish artists indeed. Perhaps when we're not so busy there might be an opportunity for me to show them to you? Now, please…sit down. There's only the three of us this evening as some of the staff are off duty, so there's no need to stand on ceremony. Moira, why don't you tell Lucy that she can serve the soup?'

As the older woman turned hurriedly away again, Georgia felt her cheeks burn with indignation beneath Keir's disconcerting scrutiny. She arranged herself in her chair. Didn't he know it was rude to stare? She swallowed hard, irritated with herself that she should let herself be so affected by the way he looked at her. She'd worked for attractive bosses in the past...of course she had. But none had bothered her sufficiently that she couldn't think a single straight thought without feeling flustered!

Reaching for her perfectly folded napkin, Georgia shook it out and laid it in her lap. 'This is such an incredible house, and the grounds—from what I've seen so far—are quite breathtaking! You must love living in such a beautiful place,' she commented conversationally.

Her blood ran cold as ice water at the look in his eyes. 'That is your assumption, is it?'

'I only meant that—'

'Don't be so quick to make careless judgements, Miss Cameron,' he advised broodingly. 'Have you not heard the adage "never judge a book by its cover"?'

CHAPTER TWO

'WHAT DO YOU MEAN?'

She found herself trapped by his glance for an almost excruciatingly long moment, and Georgia wondered what she'd said that was so wrong. There wasn't just irritation in his chastising glare. She was sensitive enough to detect some deep unhappiness there too, and for some reason her stomach turned hollow. There was such strength of will and vitality in Keir's strong, handsome face, and the idea that such an indomitable visage might be hiding some profound hurt behind it disturbed her more than she considered natural for somebody she'd only just met, and she didn't know why…

'It doesn't matter. Have you heard from Noah recently? No doubt you know he's coming for a visit next weekend?'

The swift change of subject caused her smooth brows to draw momentarily together. 'Yes, I know.

He rang me yesterday. We speak on the phone every couple of days.'

'And has he told you how he's getting along?'

Even as he asked the question Keir knew it wasn't Noah's welfare that was uppermost in his mind. He admired the younger man, of course—his professionalism, ability to work hard and deliver on a promise were commendable. But right then Keir was actually dwelling on the obviously close relationship he enjoyed with his disarming sister. To speak on the phone so often when they were away from each other was hardly something he could have imagined doing with his own brother.

He and Robbie had drifted apart many years ago—with Robbie preparing to take on the mantle of Laird after their father, with all that that entailed, and Keir leaving Glenteign just as soon as he could, to pursue his determination to go into business for himself and put his less than joyful childhood memories firmly behind him. Talking to his brother on a regular basis would only have reminded him of that dark period in his life, and Keir definitely didn't want reminders. The fact that he was back at Glenteign now, after all these years, and had inherited the role of Laird of the estate himself when he'd never wanted anything remotely to do with it again, was a twist of fate he hadn't foreseen. He was still learning to live with it…

'He seems happy enough...settling in and immersing himself in the job that has to be done.' The edges of her mouth lifting in a tentative smile, Georgia laid her hands one on top of the other in her lap, as if considering her words very carefully.

Sensing that his cutting remark had made her nervous, Keir told himself he should have been more guarded. Usually he was. After all, shielding his true feelings from others had become second nature to him since childhood.

'It was very good of you to recommend him to your friends in the Highlands,' Georgia continued. 'He's grown to love Scotland, and I know he would have found it a wrench to leave. Also, I don't think I thanked you for offering me this job of filling in for your own secretary. It's good to get out of London for a while. How is she, by the way? Your secretary, I mean?'

'Recovering slowly. It was a bad break, unfortunately, with some complications. She may have to have another operation to put it right.'

'I'm sorry to hear that.'

'That's why I needed someone who could step in and competently take over where Valerie left off. I've only been back at Glenteign for nine months myself, and what with organising the work on the gardens and getting them up to scratch again after the death of my brother... Well, there's a lot of work involved in running an estate like this and it doesn't get done by itself. Come and sit down, Moira… Is Lucy bringing the soup?'

'She'll be along directly.'

Georgia felt relief that the other woman had reappeared. Even though she'd been shocked and sympathetic to hear that Keir had so recently lost his brother, and she longed to learn more, she was also wary of saying the wrong thing again. Hunger was also gnawing at her. Fast food at a motorway service station was no substitute for good home-cooked food, and that was a fact! She was honestly looking forward to her meal.

Sitting opposite Georgia at the beautifully laid table, Moira let her friendly brown eyes focus kindly on her.

'I just wanted to tell you, lassie, that Hamish has had the food you left for him, and is now curled up by the range in the kitchen. He was looking quite content when I left him, so there's no need for you to worry. I'm sure he's going to settle in just fine!'

'Thank you. It was very good of you to see to him like that. I'm sure he's loving every bit of all the extra attention he's been receiving!'

'He's a wee lamb, that's what he is! It's lovely for us to have a dog about the place again…isn't it, Chief Strachan?'

'If you say so…' Refusing to be drawn, Keir

glanced impatiently at the doorway just as the soup arrived, carried on a large solid silver tray by a very pretty auburn-haired girl who couldn't have been much older than seventeen.

When she would have served Keir first at the head of the table—as no doubt she usually did—surprisingly he directed her down to Georgia instead.

A brief smile touched the corners of a mouth that seemed somehow reluctant to utilise that gesture too often, and his gaze was wry. 'No doubt you're only too ready for your meal after your long drive, Georgia, and we won't keep you waiting any longer to fulfil your great need!'

Although pleased by his apparent thoughtfulness, Georgia was slightly embarrassed too. Perhaps he'd seen her relieved glance at the bowls of steaming soup on the tray Lucy carried and secretly thought it unseemly somehow that a woman should so unwittingly display her hunger? She was inhabiting a whole new world of manners and formality that she wasn't used to, and she would probably have to learn to be a little less impulsive and less apt to reveal her feelings.

'Well, it smells absolutely delicious! Carrot and coriander, if I'm not mistaken?'

'That's right lassie. So...do you like to cook yourself?' Moira asked politely.

Daring a swift glance at Keir from beneath her

curling chestnut lashes, Georgia picked up her spoon, waiting for both he and Moira to do the same before she started eating. 'I've always tried to prepare fresh food for me and Noah when he's at home, and, yes, I do enjoy a bit of cooking… But it's not always possible when we're both busy working and invariably get in quite late. I usually try and do something nice at the weekends, though…like a roast on a Sunday, with a home cooked pudding to follow. Apple crumble is Noah's favourite.'

'There's not many young women of your age who know a lot about cooking in my experience,' Keir commented thoughtfully. 'Apart from your brother, do you often cook for other people?'

In the flickering candlelight, his blue eyes glowed like the glint of fireflies, and for a moment Georgia felt as if they were the only two people in the room. 'No, not really. Like I said…' Her cheeks throbbed and burned beneath his unflinching cynosure. 'I'm usually busy working…both outside and in the home.'

'Are you telling me that you don't have a social life?'

Where was this leading? Georgia wondered, a sense of panic flowing through her bloodstream. All she wanted to do was enjoy her soup and assuage her hunger—not answer too awkward questions that made her feel vaguely as if she was being interrogated.

'I see my friends, and we do the usual things—like going to the cinema or eating out… So, yes—I do have a social life.'

The fact that she hadn't done any of the above for quite some time now, because she'd been too busy working hard, worrying about finances and fretting about Noah's welfare, was Georgia's private business and not the kind of thing she would remotely want to discuss with people she'd just met…however curious.

Keir saw the slightly agitated rise and fall of her chest in the unremarkable pink dress and didn't know why he was suddenly fishing for details about her private life. He was only aware of a disturbing tension deep inside him whenever his glance happened to settle on her beautiful face, which it seemed to be doing at a rather compelling rate. He should have quizzed Noah more about his sister. He should have somehow learned that she had the ability to mesmerise with her eyes, her smile, her voice…he should have learned that she blushed easily when discomfited or embarrassed, and that her smooth, silky skin glowed like satin in the flickering candlelight… If Keir had known these things before he'd gone ahead and hired her—then he might never have agreed to her coming to Glenteign at all. Georgia Cameron was too much of a disturbing distraction. Especially when there was so much that had to be done.

As much as he didn't want to be back in the family home, now that Robbie was gone he had a responsibility to carry on in his stead. Besides that, there was also the livelihood of the staff to think of, as well as the local people in the surrounding villages who had lived and worked on this land since time immemorial and had certain expectations of their Laird.

Glenteign had been in Keir's family for generations, and now there was no one left but him—and a distant ailing uncle in Cape Town, who was hardly interested or even desirous of coming back to Scotland after spending the majority of his life tending vineyards in South Africa. Keir had to be focused and committed to the task in hand if he was going to win the respect of people who looked up to him, and he needed to inspire the help and support that was necessary to help him do that. No…it wouldn't help his case one bit to become too friendly with the bewitching Ms Cameron…

'Let's eat, shall we? Or the soup will get cold.'

Directing a final rueful glance Georgia's way, Keir deliberately diverted his attention to his meal…

Rising early the next morning, Georgia pushed the memory of last night's slightly strained atmosphere at dinner determinedly out of her head. Today was a new day, she told herself, and she and her new boss needed time to get to know each other's ways before they both relaxed their guards a little around each other and felt more comfortable.

Although she didn't think it was likely that someone with the responsibility of such a large country estate and the weight all that must place on his shoulders would ever really relax their guard around anyone.

Nevertheless, Georgia was even more determined this morning to make things work. She'd been given a great opportunity to get out of London for a while and live in the countryside, which had always been a longed-for dream, as well as earning the best salary she'd made in ages, and she wasn't going to waste even a second filling her head with self-doubt about whether she'd done the right thing or not.

Allowing her lips to curve with pleasure at the thought of being able to explore her new surroundings at her leisure on her day off, she hurriedly washed and dressed. Throwing on jeans, trainers and an old sweatshirt of Noah's that she had commandeered a long time ago, she headed off to the kitchen to collect Hamish for his walk.

The rest of the house was as silent as a church as she carefully undid the sturdy locks on the front door and stepped outside. It was a rare morning, as her dad would have said, and a fine mist clung like a draped silken cobweb over the mountain peaks that edged above the tall firs in the distance. For a disturbing moment Georgia knew a pang of longing so great that she stood stock still, with Hamish gazing expectantly up at her, her hazel eyes awash with tears.

'You'd love it here, Dad,' she whispered softly beneath her breath. 'The air is so sweet you can almost taste it.' Resolutely scrubbing away the moisture on her cheeks, she raised her chin and walked from the great house with a spring in her step. As she feasted her hungry gaze on a landscape that would stir emotion in even the stoniest of hearts, she thought how she could easily live here and never set foot in another city or town again.

Overjoyed at being outdoors, and released off his lead, Hamish bounded across the springy emerald grass and headed off towards the magnificent sentinel of trees that stood guard in front of the mountains up ahead. And as Georgia followed behind him, at a more leisurely rate, the tensions she'd experienced on her first evening at Glenteign faded away…

Back in the house an hour later, she declined the cooked breakfast that apparently Keir was enjoying in the smaller dining room, to share a pot of tea and a plate of hot buttered toast and marmalade with Moira Guthrie, in the expansive country kitchen.

As the two women sat companionably together at the family-sized pine table, the owner of Glenteign walked in.

'Georgia…I'd like a word, if I may?'

She started to rise to her feet, caught off guard by his sudden appearance and almost too aware of the innate sense of authority he brought into the room with his presence. With his lean, yet muscular build, everything he wore looked tailor-made for him…not to mention expensive. Even away from this amazing house and its vast grounds there would be an air of exclusivity about Keir Strachan that would always make him stand out from the crowd.

Suddenly Georgia's appetite disappeared, and she tucked a wayward chestnut curl behind her ear with less grace than she would have liked. 'Yes, of course.'

'When you've finished your breakfast will do. I'll be in my study. Moira will show you where it is.'

He'd gone again before she'd even voiced a reply. Sitting back down in her chair, Georgia inadvertently released a sigh.

'A word about the young Laird, my dear,' Moira said, resting her elbows on the table. 'He may come across as rather brusque at times, but he has a lot of responsibility on his shoulders. Not only is he Laird here, but he also has a business to think of. No matter what you might think he does have kindness in him, so don't judge him too quickly—will you, lassie?'

Georgia was still dwelling on what the housekeeper had told her when she stood outside Keir's study door a short while later. To her surprise he answered her knock almost straight away, and ushered her inside. Experiencing a deep jolt at the definitely masculine ambience of the imposing room she found herself in, Georgia couldn't help feeling she was somehow intruding.

Keir turned his deep blue gaze towards her.

'I trust you slept well? I know it's not always the case the first few nights in a strange house, but I'm sure you'll quickly get used to things.'

Surprisingly, Georgia *had* slept well. No doubt the long day's drive to get to Glenteign and her trepidation about what things would be like when she got there had contributed to her near exhaustion when her head had finally hit the pillow.

'Yes, I slept very well, thank you.'

'And your room is to your liking?'

'It's lovely.'

'Moira takes care of all that sort of thing…always has. She's been housekeeper here since my father's time, so if you need anything at all or want to know where anything is she's the person to ask.'

Seeing the question in her clear hazel eyes and sure he hadn't misread it, Keir held Georgia's glance with a wry twist of his lips.

'Unfortunately there's no Lady Glenteign to help exert that essential feminine influence that makes a house a home. So apart from my bedroom and this study—a room that I view strictly as my own domain—you'll no doubt see evidence of those important female touches everywhere else in the house courtesy of my housekeeper.'

Vaguely discomfited by the fact that he'd practically read her mind, Georgia moved her glance to the opened casement window opposite Keir's desk and back again. 'You mentioned last night at dinner that your brother had died? I just wanted to say how sorry I was to hear that. It must be devastating to lose someone so close in your family.'

'We weren't as close as we might have been, but, yes…it was quite awful to lose him.'

Seeing the sympathy on her concerned face, Keir felt strangely at odds admitting something so personal to a woman he'd only just met—like trying on a suit that didn't fit—and was frankly surprised that he'd allowed himself to be so uncharacteristically candid. But sometimes the pain of losing Robbie and remembering the bleak reality of their childhood was so crushing that he thought he might go mad if he didn't ever speak his feelings out loud. Yet he knew in reality that he couldn't afford to show even a hint of such weakness to anybody. In his illustrious family it just wasn't done.

'Was he married? Did he have a family of his own?' Georgia ventured.

'The answer is no, to both of those questions.

Thank you for your condolences, but I really do need to get on.'

'Right.'

He saw her own guard come up, and immediately regretted it.

'So? Presumably you wanted to talk to me about work?'

She crossed her arms over her chest in the too-large navy blue sweatshirt she wore, with its recognisable sports motif, and Keir realised that it had probably belonged to her brother at some point. The realisation immediately reminded him of how close the two of them must be, and he knew again a faint yet disturbing pang of envy.

Because Robbie was dead, and he would now never have the chance to be close to him even if he wished it, and because he'd been forced to return to Glenteign when he'd rather be a million miles away, Keir's pain spilled over into sudden irritation.

'I know it's Sunday, but we're going to have to make a start on things today. Everything's got far too behind to be left until tomorrow, so the sooner we start to tackle the backlog, the better. If you had any plans to look round the gardens or drive into the village, then I'm afraid you're going to be disappointed.'

'I didn't make any plans to go anywhere, and I'm perfectly aware that I came here to work. It's no problem for me to work on a Sunday… I've done it many times.'

'Good. Then might I suggest that you change into something a little more appropriate for work, and come back here in…' he gave a perfunctory glance at his watch '…say twenty minutes?'

'I'm only dressed like this because I took Hamish for a walk!'

'The shirt is your brother's, I take it?'

'Is that a problem?'

For a moment Keir saw mutiny in her surprised glance, and as his gaze descended from those flashing hazel eyes of hers to her softly bare mouth an unexpected jolt of sexual heat zig-zagged hotly through his insides. The sensation staggered him, arising unbidden as it did—and in what could hardly be deemed a 'provocative' situation.

'I don't have time to stand here bandying words with you, Ms Cameron… Just go and do as I say, will you?'

CHAPTER THREE

THE SLIGHTLY COOLER evening air that breezed in through the open casement windows arrested Georgia's attention with the ravishing floral scent it brought with it. Seated at the absent Valerie's desk, immersed in typing yet another long and involved letter regarding estate business, she briefly closed her eyes and inhaled deeply. The hypnotic perfume of roses in full bloom was almost soporific, and undeniably sensual as well. Lifting her arms, she stretched like a contented cat, her breasts pushing against the Indian cotton of her blouse, and the ache in her back from sitting too long eased.

'When you've finished that letter we may as well call it a day.'

Her eyes flew open again at the sound of Keir's rich, cultured tones. They'd worked alongside each other mainly in silence save for a couple of telephone calls he'd had to make, with Keir and herself only speaking when it was absolutely essential. Having been quite content with this arrangement, Georgia had to reacquaint herself with the sound of his arresting voice.

A brief surge of disturbing heat flowed through her in response, and she quickly dropped her arms and turned her head to look at him.

Having observed her unknowingly seductive stretch, and seen the points of her breasts strain the material of the soft white blouse she wore, Keir reeled from the thunderbolt of desire that shot through his insides at the sight. In fact, he'd plainly detected a husky inflection in his voice that had been the direct result of that moment of unexpected sexual excitement.

'Are you sure? I don't mind working on for another hour or so, if you need me to,' she replied.

He was sorely tempted to agree. If only to hope that he might glimpse such an unwittingly sensual little manoeuvre again… *Good God, he had been working too hard!* Suddenly impatient with himself, Keir got to his feet and swept the pile of correspondence he'd been diligently sifting through deliberately aside.

'Enough is enough,' he said gruffly, raking his fingers through his straight dark hair. 'Besides…dinner is at seven on a Sunday, and no doubt you'll want to take Hamish for a walk before you go and get ready.'

'He's not the only one who could do with a stretch of the legs.' Georgia smiled. 'I feel as if I've been welded to this chair, I've sat in it so long!'

'Finding the going too tough already? This is only the tip of the iceberg. The week ahead will be even harder.'

His mocking words completely demolished her smile.

'It's not too tough at all! I'm used to a fairly punishing pace, and I can handle it so please don't worry on that score.'

'I'm glad to hear it. Tomorrow morning we've got a hundred and one things to get through, not *least* catching up with the rest of this wretched correspondence! It seems to have grown into a veritable mountain since Valerie's accident. I also need you to liaise with Moira and the kitchen staff about a couple of dinners that I'm giving at the house which are coming up. After that I need you to familiarise yourself with the local post office in Lochheel, because I'll need you to take the post there at the end of each day, and after that...' He paused, to make sure she was keeping up with this itinerary. 'In the evening I'll need you to come with me to Dundee, where I'm attending a classical concert. It's a charity benefit, organised by a friend of mine, and as I have an invitation for two I thought you might as well come and enjoy the evening with me. Did you bring anything suitable to wear to a black-tie event?'

He was asking her to sit through an entire concert with him? Listening to some blissful classical music would not be in the least bit arduous, but spending the evening with a man who seemed not to even know the meaning of the word 'relax' definitely would! Even though they had worked together in relative peace, she had still easily sensed the tension in him. Every time he'd moved, even a little bit, he'd practically made her jump! And, reflecting quickly on the contents of the suitcase she had brought, Georgia knew straight away that she didn't possess the kind of sophisticated outfit that he was no doubt hoping she possessed to wear to this event.

'No…I'm afraid I don't,' she told him. 'I didn't expect that I'd need—'

'In that case I'll have to talk to Moira. There are a couple of vintage dresses that have been in the family for years. I'm sure there must be one in your size. I'll ask Moira to show you, and you can try them on.' His relentlessly blue eyes narrowing impatiently, Keir frowned. 'If they're not suitable then we'll just have to add shopping to our itinerary and get you something.'

Georgia's spine stiffened in protest. *She didn't want to spend money on an expensive evening dress she might never wear again just so that Keir Strachan wouldn't be embarrassed by her lack of suitable attire on just one occasion!*

'Perhaps I could just sit and wait for you outside the concert hall?' she suggested, thinking how that would be infinitely preferable to enduring a shopping trip she couldn't afford with a man who put her so on edge she would be apt to buy the first unsuitable dress she set eyes on because he distracted her so!

'Out of the question! Don't you enjoy dressing up on occasion? Most women I know don't find it such a great hardship.'

Surprised to find amusement lurking in his compelling eyes, Georgia did not smile back. 'I'm afraid I manage on quite a tight budget that doesn't run to buying lots of expensive clothes. I have a brother, a house and a dog to look after, as well as myself, and that takes quite a bit of financial juggling I can tell you!'

He was frowning again as she finished speaking, and Georgia's heart was thumping too hard inside her chest at having confessed her situation so candidly. But one thing she didn't want to do—even to save face—was pretend. In her book it was always best to tell the truth…no matter what. Her parents had drummed that fact into both her and Noah from almost as soon as they could talk.

'I agree that London can be an expensive place to live,' Keir commented. 'But isn't Noah's gardening business paying its way yet?'

'Glenteign was his first really decent commission. Every spare penny we've both earned has gone back into the business. It's early days yet, but Noah is such a brilliant designer I'm sure it won't be long before people are flocking to his door to get him to come and design their gardens!'

'Judging from what I've personally experienced of his abilities, I'm sure you're right.'

'Well...I'll just finish this letter, then I'll go and walk Hamish.'

'Georgia?'

'Yes?'

'I'm sure Moira will come up with something to save the day.'

Feeling heat rush into her cheeks at the unexpected kindness in his voice, Georgia turned her attention back to her typing.

Watching her slender fingers fly across the keyboard at a rate that was definitely impressive, Keir silently acknowledged that so far everything that Noah had said about his sister's secretarial skills was true. She'd coped with everything he had thrown at her today, and she hadn't flapped...not *once. He regretted it if he'd embarrassed her about a dress for the benefit concert, but he'd appreciated her candour.* Not many people would have had the guts to tell him the truth about their finances—and without any sense of feeling hard done by either, just simply stating facts.

'Good. That's settled, then.'

Going to the door, he stood there for at least half a minute, staring at the way her long chestnut hair curled so provocatively at the ends and remembering the way her flimsy cotton blouse had outlined her very arresting figure as she'd stretched. By the time Keir turned away to leave the room he found himself to be in a state of highly aroused tension, and the only sensible thing to do to alleviate it was to put some distance between his new secretary and himself as quickly as possible…

'And where are you off to this fine morning, my dear?'

Keir's friendly housekeeper waylaid Glenteign's newest employee as she was about to get into her car the next morning. The day was seasonably warm and bright, and Georgia was wearing a dark lime cotton sweater with white tapered linen trousers, very conscious since his remark about Noah's shirt not to appear too casual for her employer's liking.

Pushing her sunglasses onto the top of her head, she smiled, already feeling very much at home with the older woman.

'I'm off to Lochheel. I need to go to the post office for the Chief. He was going to take me himself, but he's got several phone calls to make this morning and can't spare the time.'

The truth of it was—because he'd definitely got out of the wrong side of the bed this morning, judging by his extremely tetchy mood—Georgia was glad to be going on her own. It would also give her a chance to enjoy some of the spectacular countryside without having to make stilted conversation with her new boss.

'That's usually the way of it...' Moira sighed. 'The man just always has so much to do! Considering he's scarcely been Laird here for two minutes, it's an absolute credit to his skill and dedication that he's already achieved so much!'

Georgia frowned, thinking. 'So his brother was Laird here before him? Is that right?'

'Until he was killed in that terrible car accident in America...yes, he was. Nobody thought that Keir would ever come back here again...even for a visit! But Robbie's death changed everything for him.' The kind brown eyes of the other woman crinkled with concern around the edges for a moment, as if she'd inadvertently revealed more than she should have. 'Look at me, standing here chatting away when I need to get on! Enjoy your drive to Lochheel, lassie. No doubt I'll see you again later.'

For a few moments, as the housekeeper bustled away to get on with her own busy tasks, Georgia stood stock still on the gravel drive beside her car, her mind captured by what Moira had said about nobody thinking that Keir would ever come back to Glenteign and how his brother's death had changed everything for him. Was that why he had warned her during their first dinner together that she should not be so quick to make 'careless judgements'?

Having clearly assumed that he must love living at Glenteign, Georgia was now getting the distinct impression that he didn't, and that there were good reasons why he didn't… But how tragic—to live in such an amazing place, with all the advantages that most people could only fantasise about, and yet secretly wish you were somewhere else.

Sometimes the ironies of life just got to her—they really did. There was Georgia, living in a small cramped house in Hounslow, directly beneath the flight path of the planes out of Heathrow, struggling to keep her head above water, dreaming of the peace and quiet of a place like this and wishing that money wasn't such an issue. And there was Keir, living with the complete antithesis of her own situation and yet apparently deeply unhappy. How was anybody supposed to make sense of it all?

Shaking herself out of her reverie, she got into the car, briefly studied the map she'd left on the seat, then gunned the engine and drove off. Although she would take great pleasure in enjoying the scenery as she drove, she would find Lochheel and locate the post office as quickly as she could—then get back to

Glenteign to at least try and alleviate some of the burden of work that was clearly getting her new boss down…

They'd scarcely taken a moment to even glance at the cups of tea Moira had brought them at varying intervals that afternoon, they'd both worked so hard. Now, as Georgia sat in front of the elegant Victorian mirror on her dressing table and applied a deep plum lipstick, she told herself she was feeling far less tense at the idea of accompanying Keir to the classical concert than she had been earlier.

Working alongside him, seeing how effortlessly he seemed to get the measure of situations and handle them, how diplomatic and concerned he could be when addressing more sensitive issues presented to him both by letter and on the telephone, there was much to admire about the man. And that was apart from his brilliantly azure eyes and his firm, handsome jaw…

Catching the flare of her own dark pupils reflected back at her, Georgia momentarily stilled, her fingers gripping the slim metal case of her lipstick and her cheeks suffusing with heat.

Years of celibacy must have made my mind deranged if I can think for even one minute that he and I could—

She shut off the thought abruptly, already too disturbed by the erotic image that presented itself so temptingly in her mind, dropped her lipstick into her make-up bag, and pushed to her feet.

Crossing over to the bed, to fetch the black-fringed Spanish-style evening shawl that Moira insisted went with the dramatic black evening dress she'd borrowed for the evening, she almost jumped through the roof at the loud knock that sounded at the door.

'Georgia, lassie?'

It was Moira herself. Sighing with pure relief, Georgia put her hand to her chest to still the sudden disconcerting surge of her heartbeat. For one dreadful moment there she'd thought it might be Keir. She felt quite a different person in the beautiful borrowed dress, and she needed some time to compose herself before she faced her boss. She picked up her purse.

'The Chief is waiting for you outside in the car,' the housekeeper continued cheerfully. 'He asked me to come and tell you to please hurry up!'

In the middle of Barber's *Adagio for Strings*—a piece of music that always reminded him that the things of this world were ultimately fragile and did not last, Keir glanced at his companion's rapt profile and experienced a searing stab of need so great that it actually caused his heart to race.

Georgia Cameron looked so stunning that she

provoked powerful stirrings of desire and longing in Keir that he could not ignore. Neither had he been blind to the admiring glances that had come her way when they'd walked into the early nineteenth-century building that was housing the concert tonight. And it was perfectly true that his male ego knew a certain sense of pride at being her escort.

Her compelling dark beauty highlighted the impact of the dramatic black satin dress she wore even more and Keir could not imagine that anyone had looked half as arresting in it before. Whoever had first bought it had had good taste, though. The black dress had an ultra-feminine style that was definitely from the 1930s or 1950s, and it was subtly sexy in a way that most twenty-first-century women's clothing was not. Its nipped-in waist made the most of Georgia's womanly curves, and the elegant neckline exposed flawless skin that no beauty product could hope to emulate in a million years.

Keir wondered if Georgia even guessed at the riveting impression both she and the dress were making on the people around them. Several of his acquaintances who were in the audience this evening had glanced their way with frank curiosity many times after Keir and Georgia had left their company to circulate the room—when they'd thought he wasn't aware of them looking. They were all too polite to suggest openly that his stunning companion might be a bit more than just his temporary secretary, and the normally intensely private Keir found to his surprise that for once he didn't actually mind the silent speculation that was going on.

Since his return, gossip in the local community had been rife about whom he was or was not dating. Although he was a well-travelled businessman, there was an unspoken preference around Glenteign that any girlfriend of the Laird should definitely hail from closer to home. The older folk especially were always hoping for a wedding, and for the young Laird to settle down with his eventual new wife and start a family. They had been disappointed when Robbie had not been able to achieve that, and now naturally they expected Keir to do what his brother had not. That was the way of it when you lived amongst a community steeped in history and tradition. *It was a ball and chain that he could live without…*

That was why, when it had come to looking at some new fresh designs for the formal gardens, Keir had deliberately chosen a young, innovative designer like Noah Cameron, instead of someone more obviously traditional. It was important to move with the times. And, no matter what his respect for what had gone before, he was his own man and would *not* be dictated to as to how he should run the estate by *anyone.*

As the sweetly sensual fragrance Georgia wore

caused another flare of acute electricity to silently implode inside him Keir had to secretly attest to a fascination for her that seemed to be gathering strength as the evening went on…

During the interval, as he accepted a glass of champagne from a black-tied waiter and Georgia selected sparkling mineral water instead, Keir endeavoured to find them a more private corner in the crowded room.

Above them, suspended from the high, ornate ceiling, was a rather spectacular chandelier, its crystal teardrops shimmering like the most fabulous diamonds. To add to the indisputable grandeur that surrounded them, the walls were covered in portraits of illustrious Victorians with—it had to be said—expressions that had little joy in them.

'How are you enjoying the concert?'

For a few moments her interested glance seemed to alight on everything else in the sumptuously beautiful room but *him*—as though all the treasures it held had to be given the proper time and consideration they deserved.

'Do you know what a gift you've given me tonight?' Her green-gold eyes were shining. 'The music just swept me away! In my opinion doctors should prescribe classical concerts at least once a month rather than Prozac…then I'm sure most of the population wouldn't be half so depressed!'

Her words were so passionate and her eyes glowed with such intensity of emotion that Keir could find nothing to say for the moment. He simply stared. Rarely did he meet anyone who expressed their love of the arts so vociferously. *What would it be like to have a relationship with such a woman?*

He had dated many women over the years, but had never enjoyed a true connection—a deep bond of mind, body and soul—with any of them. Keir knew that the fault more than likely lay with him. He had got too used to covering up his true feelings and was just not capable of sharing the real man behind the mask, with anyone.

'I'm sure you're right—although the National Health Service would soon be bankrupt if they did!'

His smile was genuinely amused, but the gesture did not fully reach his compelling blue eyes, Georgia saw. The tenuous nature of it underlined her opinion that being wealthy did not help keep the psychological discomfort of life away. She couldn't help wondering what demons dogged him. The loss of his brother had to be one, but what were the others?

Georgia intimately knew what her own were: the fear of something dreadful happening to her or Noah, losing their house, becoming sick and not being able to work. And ending up alone…that was a biggie. She sighed, not liking the sudden wave of melancholy that engulfed her when only moments ago she'd been so elated.

'I read a quote somewhere that most people's troubles arise from the fact that they can't sit alone in a room in silence. Maybe they're afraid to face what might come up? It's probably like stirring a great soup…you don't know what might rise to the surface…and that's why people have to stay busy to distract themselves. What do you think?'

'We live in a world of commerce and achieving. We don't all have the time to sit and contemplate our navels.'

His caustic comment privately pained her, but even so Georgia could tell that her reflections had disturbed Keir.

'Well, then…it's just as well that sometimes we're fortunate to have opportunities like tonight—to sit and listen to sublime music that feeds the spirit and helps us contemplate other things besides the world of commerce!' There was deliberate challenge in her tone. 'I for one would go mad if I wasn't able to find some peace somewhere!'

Georgia had seen how moved Keir had been by the music, even though he might hurry to deny it. She would have registered his response even if she *hadn't* turned briefly to glance at his riveted profile. The emotional tension in him had been *palpable.* It had made Georgia aware that there were hidden depths to this serious-minded businessman and Laird, and driven her to speculate that perhaps he *did* possess a *less harsh and guarded* side. A side he was determined not to expose to the world. *Was he afraid of being hurt somehow?* It was a *provocative* idea, even though Georgia told herself she'd be a fool to explore it any further.

'Yes—peace. I suppose that's ultimately what we all want.' Surprisingly, he acquiesced, 'So tell me…what other things besides music do you enjoy?'

'Oh, there isn't any lack of occupations. It's just having the time to do them that's the problem.'

'For instance?'

'Well…' Georgia's smile was as disarming as that of a little girl who'd just been told she was to be a bridesmaid for the first time. 'Reading is a great passion—I love to lose myself in a good book… I also enjoy a bit of gardening myself from time to time…tiny though our little plot is! I also love hiking and swimming and going to the movies. Can I have a couple more?' She sucked in a deep breath and laughed. 'Taking long rambling walks with Hamish, and—finally!—spending time with my brother of course.'

'You must be greatly looking forward to seeing him at the weekend.'

'Oh, yes!' Her eyes sparkled with undisguised longing. 'I've missed him very much!'

Keir was mesmerised by the animation in her face.

'How long has it been since you last saw him?'

'At least three months. He came back home one weekend at the end of May for a brief visit. You were in New York on business—I remember him telling me.'

Keir remembered too. He'd been meeting with officials regarding Robbie's car accident. His rental car had been hit side-on by a drunken driver. He hadn't had a chance of saving himself. Keir's gut clenched hard as iron.

'Have you and Noah always been so close?' he asked, the pain ebbing a little as he forced himself to concentrate on Georgia's answer.

'We lost our parents one after the other in the same year. Noah was fourteen and I was just five years older. We have no other living family, so I was determined to take care of us both.'

Her cheeks had turned an impassioned pink, and Keir absorbed what she had told him with a sense of shock—for a moment his own pain at the memory of Robbie's death was banished.

'That was an amazingly brave thing to do at nineteen,' he said with admiration.

Georgia's eyebrows flew up to her hairline. 'It wasn't brave at all! What else would I have done? Let them take him away from me? My own little brother? Let him go to strangers who wouldn't love him like I do?' Her hazel eyes sparkled with unshed tears. 'I could never have lived with myself if I'd done that!

And my parents would have turned in their graves! Families should stick together…especially when times are tough. Don't you agree?'

CHAPTER FOUR

THERE WAS NO DOUBT in Keir's mind that she meant emotionally and not just physically. But since his own parents had never been there for him or his brother in that way he could not immediately give Georgia an answer.

His mother had drunk herself to death when Keir was just eleven—no doubt to escape the foul black tempers of his father which had become increasingly worse and more threatening as the years had gone on.

Robbie had been terrified of the old man, and Keir had defied him as much as he'd been able to—he'd worn the bruises to prove it—but nothing had made any difference to how James Strachan treated his sons. Not until he'd become ill himself and seen the gates of death beckoning. By which time, of course, it had all been too late. How Moira Guthrie had stayed working for such a man—never mind nursing him after he'd got ill—Keir had never understood. He'd asked her once, and her reply had frankly stunned him.

'I saw that he had good in him,' she had asserted, in her quiet yet forthright way, and Keir had had to acquiesce that the woman had far more forbearance and forgiveness in her than he could ever hope to have.

For himself, he couldn't ever foresee a time when he would be able to forgive James Strachan his transgressions. The man had simply not been fit to be a father.

A muscle throbbing at the side of his temple, Keir grimaced before answering Georgia's question. 'In an ideal world I suppose families should stick together,' he remarked. 'But as we both know this world is far from ideal, and people who have no business even contemplating having children sadly do, and screw up their kids' lives as well as their own.'

And God only knew what pretty Georgia Cameron with her passionate adherence to family loyalty and love would have made of his completely unnatural family! He shuddered to think.

'Ladies and gentlemen, would you please find your seats as the concert will resume in three minutes' time...'

Relieved by the instruction that meant their conversation had to come to an end—because it was touching upon things that made him uneasy—Keir inclined his head briefly towards his companion. 'Time to get back.'

'Yes.'

Seeing a look that might have been concern in her pretty eyes and steeling himself against it, Keir took Georgia's glass, deposited it beside his own and, unable to resist the opportunity to touch her, put his hand beneath her elbow to steer her back towards their seats.

'All the worry and stress has gone from your eyes.'

'Has it?'

Her relaxed stroll coming to a stop on one of the myriad footpaths throughout the gardens, Georgia turned to regard her tall, blond, blue-eyed brother, and couldn't suppress the effervescent bubble of happiness that rose up inside her at the sight of him.

He'd arrived at Glenteign only last night for the weekend and she had been thrilled to see a familiar, smiling face.

'This place has done wonders for you…I can see that.' Looking thoughtful, Noah reached out and fingered a curling tendril of her chestnut hair. 'You're a different girl…and you've lost that grey London pallor!'

'Who wouldn't love it here?'

Turning slightly away from him, Georgia leant

forward to smell the scent of a drowsy yellow rose, drooping heavily on its stem beside the footpath. The path was resplendent on all sides with foliage, plants and flowers—some past their best, since September was swiftly approaching, but still lovely all the same.

Roses had always been her favourite. She supposed it was because her mother had loved them so, and had always brought one or two into the house from the garden to light up a room when she was feeling a little melancholy. Even though she and Noah had been on their own for years now, Georgia still found it hard sometimes to realise that their mother was no longer there…her father too. They had been such wonderful, loving parents.

For some reason just at that moment the memory crept into her mind of what Keir had said at the concert. Something about not living in an ideal world, and how some people should never have children because they not only screwed up their own lives but their kids' as well. Was that what had happened to Keir and his brother Robbie?

Her brow creased with renewed concern. She'd already concluded that the Laird of Glenteign was not exactly the happiest of men. Sometimes she glimpsed such singular sadness in his riveting blue eyes that she longed to be able to banish it for good… But she knew it was a very dangerous impulse, and one that should definitely be curbed if she didn't want to find herself not just hurt but out of a job too…

'And what about the Highlands? What about where you're working now?' she asked Noah, determined to focus on her brother's visit above all else while he was there. 'Do you like it as much as Glenteign?'

'Oh, it's beautiful enough, all right—and the couple I'm working for are very down-to-earth…despite being landed gentry! But I enjoyed perhaps some of the best months of my life working here.' Noah lapsed into a reflective stroll again and Georgia joined him. 'Keir was great to work for. Easy to discuss my ideas with, and very fair. I enjoyed his company. How are you finding him, Georgie?'

'Oh…' She shrugged to deflect attention from the hectic colour that she knew had rushed into her cheeks at the mention of her boss. 'There were a few awkward moments at first, but now we're getting along just fine. He's off to New York on business again on Monday, so we've been very busy the past few days trying to do as much as possible before he goes.'

It was odd, but when Keir had announced the day after the benefit concert that he was going away, Georgia's stomach had turned strangely hollow. No one she'd ever worked for had had such a peculiar effect on her before.

'Oh, well… You'll enjoy being your own boss for a while, won't you?'

'Yes, I'm sure I will.'

Georgia wondered what Noah would think if he knew that the big masculine study where they worked together already seemed strangely desolate even with the idea of Keir not being there with her. The man was such a presence that the big house would not seem the same without him.

'Anyway…' Linking her arm in his, Georgia grinned. 'Guess what's for dessert at dinner tonight, in your honour?'

'Not apple crumble?'

'I asked Moira if she could arrange it as a special treat.'

'Be still my beating heart!'

Keir heard the laughter from the open study window and, drawn there away from the sheaf of legal documents he'd been busy perusing at his desk—he glanced out over the ledge towards the ground below. His heart gave a jolt at the sight of Georgia in a white summer dress, her shining chestnut hair arranged in a loose, girlish ponytail. She looked very young and carefree. Beside her was her brother, and together they made an eye-catching pair, the striking blond Noah and his darker, bewitching sister.

A slash of envy curled almost painfully in the pit of Keir's stomach. They might have lost their parents, but he could see that the bond between them was an extremely close and affectionate one. Again he thought of Robbie, and how the distance between him and his brother had grown ever wider over the years. Back at Glenteign—the root of all his early misery and pain—Keir had never felt more emotionally isolated than he did right at that moment. The sight of Georgia and Noah's delight in seeing each other merely reconfirmed that he'd made the right decision in electing to go to New York on business.

The matter that called him there was hardly urgent—he had good people working for him, who were quite capable of dealing with it—but Keir found he was glad of the excuse to go away again for a while. Being around Georgia Cameron was just unsettling him far too much, and perhaps with some real distance between them he might get things back into perspective. She was only at Glenteign temporarily, until the dependable Valerie recovered from her injury and came back. It wasn't wise to get too used to having her here, and in New York there was a girl Keir had met on his last trip. He'd vaguely promised to get in touch with her on his return…

* * *

After Noah and Kier had left, Georgia was greatly unsettled. To alleviate the restlessness that had come upon her, after work each day, and at the weekend, she walked for miles with Hamish, exploring and enjoying her breathtaking surroundings.

One day, after scrabbling over some challenging rocky crags, her back damp with perspiration and her clothes sticking to her beneath her waterproof—while Hamish had made comparatively light work of the same arduous climb beside her—she came upon a shining silvery loch, exquisitely positioned amidst tall pines. It was like discovering paradise… The sight so undid her that Georgia immediately burst into tears when she saw it.

Sitting back on a rock, she put her arms around Hamish and held him there, her gaze enthralled. She was moved almost unbearably by the spectacular scene in front of her. Did Keir ever come up here? she speculated. If he didn't, then he should. Surely the sight of all this wild, unfettered beauty would have the power to chase away all his heartache? Her own heart turned over at the memory of his strong, serious face, and she sincerely hoped that whatever he was doing in New York he might find some comfort there from the worries that beset him.

Perhaps there was a woman there who might

provide that comfort? The thought was like the viper in the Garden of Eden.

'No!'

Hamish pulled away from her in surprise. She hadn't meant to voice her disapproval out loud, and Georgia was shocked by her own unrestrained outburst.

'What am I saying?' she muttered crossly, getting to her feet and wiping loose grass from her corduroy jeans. 'He means nothing to me other than that I just work for the man! I have no right to be jealous if he's seeing some fabulously beautiful woman in New York! Why should I care? Come on Hamish…time to get back! We don't want to be late for dinner!'

Determinedly banishing thoughts of Keir from her mind, she started to negotiate the climb back down the rocks again. But a melancholy had descended that she couldn't shake, and it stayed with her for the rest of the day until she went to bed later that evening…

A few days later, the sultry weather they'd been having finally broke at around ten to midnight. An almighty crack of thunder vented its fury above the turreted rooftops of Glenteign, and Georgia sat up in bed in shock as a streak of lightning lit up the room, briefly and eerily illuminating all the previously dark corners and making her clutch at the thin cotton sheet which was all the covering her overheated body could bear.

She had a love/hate relationship with thunderstorms. While she had a secret admiration for the passion and fury they displayed, which reminded her that no matter what humankind achieved it could *not* control the elements, they frightened her deeply. Of course she'd never displayed that fear to Noah—not when he was young and had naturally relied on her to help him feel secure. But when she was on her own, as she was now, it was hard to keep her anxiety completely at bay.

She'd suffered an agony of tension all day because she'd known that a storm was threatening, and she'd guessed it would come tonight. And while Georgia despised the fear that it evoked in her, which she couldn't entirely control, she found herself wishing that Keir was at least at home, in his room down the hall from hers. It would have given her a measure of security just to know that he was there. But Keir was still in New York, and she had received no word as to when he would be returning.

Something that sounded vaguely like a door opening and closing broke into her consciousness. But as the rain started to lash with some ferocity at the casement windows with their lavish undrawn curtains Georgia wondered if she'd imagined it. Her ears strained for a repetition of the sound, or some follow-up to it, but all she heard was the rain pounding relentlessly at everything it touched. She let out her breath slowly and forced herself to try and relax.

All of a sudden she was certain she heard someone walking about in the corridor outside, and her heart leapt into her mouth. *Was it Moira?* But the housekeeper's room was on the floor below hers. What reason would she have for coming up here in the middle of the night? A new, more terrifying thought occurred.

What if they were being burgled? What if the sound she'd heard hadn't been a door innocently being opened and then closed by one of the staff, but the sound of someone breaking into the house instead?

What better distraction than a fierce thunderstorm to drown out any sound of broken glass caused by climbing through a downstairs window or breaking and entering through a side door somewhere?

Trembling hard, Georgia shoved the cotton sheet aside and slid smoothly and quietly out of bed. Switching on her lamp, dim light flooded the room. That at least reassured her. Reaching for the thin pink robe hanging over the end of the brass bedstead, she pulled it on over her bare body and swiftly tied the belt. Then, tiptoeing across the carpet, she reached for the iron poker that lay in the old-fashioned fireplace. Surprised at how heavy it was, clutching it between her hands as though it were some kind of broadsword, she crossed the room slowly to the door.

She didn't know exactly what she intended to do, or how on earth she was supposed to deal with some burly thug bent on thieving something valuable—she only knew that this was Keir's *home* that was being violated whilst he was away, and that Moira and the other staff slept on oblivious downstairs. Clearly someone had to do something!

The sound of footsteps was no more, but she thought she heard a muttered expletive—a man's voice, low and harsh. Georgia's heart began to pound so hard that to her sensitive hearing the sound drowned out the noise of the heavy rain that was pelting the windows. *Oh, dear God...* Muttering a swift prayer for help, she turned the doorknob and wrenched open the door. The light from her bedside lamp escaped into the darkened corridor and cast an eerie yellow glow.

'Just what the hell do you think you're doing?' she demanded, her gaze latching with fright onto the six-feet-plus frame of the menacing individual hovering outside Keir's bedroom door.

'I might ask you the same bloody question!' came back the irritated and furious reply.

'Keir!'

'If I were you, Georgia, I'd put down that extremely lethal looking poker before you drop it on your foot and break a couple of bones!'

'I thought you were a burglar!'

'You thought *what?*' His hard handsome face was glistening with moisture from the rain, and his jacket and trousers were darkened in several places from the spreading damp. Keir's disbelieving blue eyes regarded Georgia as though she was deranged.

Her heart slowing to a more normal beat, she pushed still shaking fingers through her tousled dark hair, her relief too immense to be measured. 'You should have rung to let us know that you were coming home!' she said accusingly.

'Why?'

Studying her with a mockingly sensual grin, Keir let his gaze drop deliberately to the thin, inadequate robe that was clearly outlining the very feminine contours of Georgia's body. Of course he must know that underneath it she was naked.

'Are you telling me that you missed me?'

What a question! Her gaze cleaving to the darkly brooding expression on his hard-hewn features, Georgia felt as if her breath had been suddenly snatched from her lungs. She'd missed his presence, yes... But surely not in the way he was implying? She quickly laid the heavy poker down on the casement windowsill beside her, as though it were now something distasteful, and curled her fingers into the flimsy edges of her robe around the neckline. Her skin was hot and prickling beneath his mocking regard.

'You're the owner of this house… I'm sure—I'm sure everybody notices it when you're not here.'

'That's not what I asked, and you know it!'

Impatiently Keir threw off his sodden jacket, uncaring where it landed, and scraped his hand through his equally damp dark hair as if too furious to contain his rage.

'And if I *had* been a burglar, what exactly did you think you could do against some threatening thug twice your size? Even *with* a poker? You could have got yourself killed or badly injured! Didn't it occur to you to phone the police if you suspected someone was breaking in? Dear Lord! Don't you have any common sense?'

An explosive crash of thunder overhead leached the colour from Georgia's already pale face. Coupled with the tension that was already holding her stomach in a vice, it made hot, frustrated tears spring readily to her eyes.

'Stop shouting at me! I was scared—scared of who you might be, *and* of this hateful storm!'

Needing to get away, Georgia fled back into her room and slammed the door behind her. *Awful, horrible, ingrate!* It would have served him bloody well right if burglars had ransacked the whole house and stolen everything he held dear!

But even as the tears started to roll down her cheeks, the door opened behind her and Keir came into the room. Georgia turned and clutched at her robe in shock. She watched dry-mouthed as he carefully closed the door again, his straight, broad-shouldered physique seeming to suck up all the oxygen in the room with its indomitable presence, leaving her very little left to breathe. The expression in his eyes was not one she recognised either.

'You should have said you were frightened of the storm.' His voice was gruff but not in an unkind way.

Georgia's heartbeat skittered.

'Are you crying?' he demanded.

Before she could reply, he strode up in front of her and touched the palm of his hand to her damp cheek. With the pad of his thumb he brushed away the slippery track of a tear and his warm breath drifted over her. *Had she ceased breathing?* It certainly seemed as if she had. Her senses held in thrall by his touch, the storm that raged outside all but forgotten, Georgia gulped down air and exhaled raggedly.

Keir's chin, with its hard, masculine cleft, was just inches from her forehead, and she had to look up to meet his searching gaze…

Staring into her mesmerising tear-filled eyes was like seeing the sun glinting gold above the green of the Glens… Her exquisitely feminine scent seemed to saturate his senses, and Keir hardly dared move lest he somehow shatter something irretrievable.

He'd stayed away longer than he'd needed to in New York because of this woman. In the couple of days following their attendance at the concert he had found it almost impossible to be in the same room as Georgia without needing to touch her. His desire had almost grown into a compulsion. She'd drawn his gaze wherever she went, and he'd barely been able to concentrate on the work that had to be done. It was a distraction he'd found hard to deal with. That was why he had grabbed at the chance to go to New York. But even when he'd been an ocean away she had dominated his thoughts. Now, home again, he realised that this budding attraction was developing into something nearer to obsession.

'There's no need to be afraid. The storm won't hurt you *or* this house. Can you imagine how many storms Glenteign has endured over the years? In an hour or so it will have blown itself out, and everything will be calm again.'

'You probably think I'm behaving like a complete coward!' Her mouth quivered, and Keir's hungry glance latched onto it as though it were heavenly perfection itself.

'Don't be ridiculous!' Even though his tone was gently mocking, he smiled and moved his fingers through the soft fall of her hair. 'You? A *coward?* You could have done someone some serious damage with that poker because you thought they were breaking in!'

'I wouldn't have used it!' Georgia looked aghast for a moment. 'Maybe I was being more stupid than brave, now that I come to think of it.'

'Why did you do it?'

'Because I didn't want anyone stealing anything of importance to you,' Georgia replied quietly, swallowing hard.

'Nothing I own would be worth risking your life for, Georgia.' His voice lowered tenderly, and Keir tipped up her chin, intent on nothing else but to fulfil the compelling, growing need inside him to feel her soft, inviting lips opening beneath his own.

As her warm sweet breath feathered invitingly across his mouth, there was a loud knock at the door.

'Georgia? Are you all right, lassie? I heard a noise from up here and thought you might be up and about because you were worried by the storm.'

'Damn!' Cursing harshly, Keir stepped away from Georgia, a sudden irresistible need to break something flashing through him with almost violent demand.

'It's Moira,' Georgia said, her expression torn. She unconsciously moistened her lips with her tongue and made Keir suffer the agony of heightened frustration—because he could not enjoy the same delectable privilege.

'Yes…I heard.'

She saw both exasperation and resignation written across his riveting features. She hurried past him to open the door, unable to deny her own frustration that Moira should choose that exact moment to check if she was all right.

The incredible realisation that she'd *wanted* Keir to kiss her flooded through her. How much had she craved the touch of his mouth on hers when the opportunity had presented itself? Even now her body still had tremors flooding through it because he had touched his palm to her cheek.

'Moira…hello,' she said, smiling awkwardly at the housekeeper, who was standing there in her long plaid dressing gown with her silver hair in curlers.

Georgia caught hold of the edge of the door and pulled it closed behind her as she joined Moira in the corridor. Apart from the occasional flash of lightning reflected in the casement windows, the area was plunged into near darkness. *What on earth would Moira think if Keir should come out of her room right now?* She prayed he wouldn't expose her like that and make the housekeeper suspect the worst. Over the past few days Georgia had come to set a lot of store by the other woman's friendship and respect. Alienating her because she thought something might be going on between her and Keir would not be good at all…

'I'm perfectly all right, thanks. I thought I heard a noise too, and I went out into the corridor to investigate, that's all.' Shrugging her slim shoulders guiltily, Georgia started to explain what had happened. She despised the need for subterfuge of any kind. It wasn't in her nature to be dishonest, and this didn't sit well with her.

'And when I came back in, the wind must have made the door slam. Maybe that was the sound you heard?'

'Aye…that must be it, then. Well, as long as you're all right. This storm is enough to put the fear of God into anybody!' Moira replied.

'They've always made me a little jumpy,' Georgia agreed.

Her back was sticky with perspiration and prickly heat at the knowledge that Keir was waiting in her room, and she worked hard at containing her anxiety and not arousing any suspicion from the other woman that something else might be bothering her aside from the weather.

'Please, Moira…go back to bed. Thank you for your concern, but I'm honestly fine. I'll see you in the morning.'

'Goodnight then, my dear.'

As the housekeeper turned away to return down

the darkened corridor to the grand curving staircase at the bottom, Georgia touched her hand to her forehead and was not surprised when it came away moist. Biting her lip, she turned the catch on the door and went back inside the room.

Keir was standing with his back to her at the window, seemingly engrossed in watching the torrential downpour that was sheeting the glass and everything else in sight. Hearing her come in, he immediately sought her out, his blue eyes as piercing as any bright searchlight.

'She's gone,' he remarked soberly.

'Yes.' Georgia stared at him, her brow furrowing. 'You don't think she heard us talking, do you?'

CHAPTER FIVE

'AND DISCOVERED THAT the Laird was home again and up to no good in his secretary's bedroom?' His smile was taunting. 'No, Georgia… I don't think she heard us. And even if she did… Moira Guthrie is the soul of discretion and wouldn't bat an eyelid.'

He'd been kind before, when he'd thought she was afraid of the storm, and he'd been going to kiss her, Georgia thought a little forlornly. But now his mood seemed to be altering…almost as if he blamed *her* for Moira knocking at the door!

'How was it that you arrived home so late?' she asked, needing to say something to ease the palpable tension between them.

'I got a flight out of Newark at the last minute. I'd concluded my business earlier in the day and simply decided to come home.'

He walked towards her, his expression as impenetrable as the rugged stone that made up the impressive walls of his ancestral home. 'For the first time in my life I actually looked forward to coming back here…did you know that?'

'Really?'

She dropped her chin and stared at the floor. A wave of heat swept upwards through her body in a dizzying rush. What was he saying?

'Why have you never looked forward to coming home before?' she asked quietly, hardly daring to move in case he denied her the answer. An answer she found she very much longed to know.

'There was nobody here that I wanted to see before.' He shrugged, his mouth twisting wryly at one corner.

'Not even your brother?' Georgia asked the question even while all her senses were in uproar at what he'd just confessed.

'I told you we weren't close.'

A dark look had crept into his eyes.

'Why weren't you close?' Her voice was barely above a whisper. 'Did you have a fight or something?'

A muscle visibly showed itself contracting in the dark shadow of his sculpted cheekbone. 'No…we didn't have a fight. The tension between me and Robbie was an unspoken thing.'

'And you weren't able to heal that tension before he died? Is that it? Is that why you seem so troubled?'

'It might be late, Georgia, but trust me—this isn't the time for night-time confessions! Especially the kind that are apt to make me want to leave this cursed place again.'

'I don't want you to leave.'

'What did you say?' Appearing startled, Keir stared and Georgia could have bitten out her tongue. Why on earth had she come out with that? But she really didn't want him to leave again... She just didn't want him to get the wrong impression about what she'd said and why she'd said it.

'What a night you chose to return!' she declared, deliberately trying to lighten the atmosphere.

'I know...and I'm sorry if I gave you a fright.'

Surprising her, Keir reached out to touch her, and as his hard, warm fingers curled round her chin to raise it she was seized by such trembling that she could barely conceal it from him.

'Next time I'll be sure and ring you to let you know that I'm coming home,' he promised, his voice threaded with a hushed and sensual undertone that riveted her.

'Maybe next time you go away I'll be back in London because I won't be working here any more.'

'Are you in such a hurry to leave me, Georgia?' His tone was slightly mocking and his grip tightened a little around her chin.

'It's not that... It's just that Valerie will be back sooner or later, and I—'

'You have a life in London, waiting for you… I know.' His voice threaded with apparent dissatisfaction, he dropped his hands down to his sides. Immediately Georgia felt bereft of his touch, as if some integral part of her had suddenly been ripped away.

'Does that include a man, perhaps?' he demanded.

Shadows seemed to shift in his penetrating glare, and Georgia wished she could look away—but she couldn't.

His question threw her into a state of near panic. If he knew…if he even *guessed* how little experience she'd had of intimate relationships he probably wouldn't be able to believe it. He might mock her, or simply conclude she must be lying.

Fiddling with the neckline of her skimpy cotton robe, she was certain her lack of experience must show. Because it was so hard to contain her reaction to him and keep it hidden neatly away, like a secret letter stowed amongst her personal things in a bedroom drawer. His nearness was making her feel as if she stood too close to a scorching fire, yet at the same time she desired it above all else…

'You're right. This isn't the moment for night-time confessions, and I really think you should go now. We both need to go to bed… I mean to go to sleep… In our—in our own beds is what I mean!' Her face went beetroot red at the hash she was making of what should have been a simple statement.

In response, Keir looked grim. There was certainly no amusement evident at her clumsy phrasing.

'I had better go, then,' he announced clearly. 'Before I finish what I started to do before my loyal housekeeper knocked on the door and ruined everything. An event that with hindsight you will probably no doubt welcome!'

He left her then, shutting the door with deliberately firm emphasis behind him, and Georgia stood frozen for a full minute, locked in the myriad emotions that welled up inside her. She no longer felt afraid of the storm that vented its fury outside because her head was too full of wild, heated thoughts to be fully aware of much else but her own disquiet.

Keir was wrong about her welcoming the interruption from his housekeeper...so wrong.

'Good morning, Moira.'

'Georgia, my dear!'

The friendly housekeeper glanced up from the cooking range as the younger woman entered the large bright kitchen. Immediately she observed the telling signs of a sleepless night on Georgia's slightly paler than usual face.

'You look like you had as restless a night as I had,

love. Goodness gracious, but that was some hullabaloo last night, wasn't it? Come and sit down, lassie, and I'll make you a nice rejuvenating cup of tea.'

'Thanks, I'd really appreciate that… And I'm sorry if I added to your sleepless night with that slamming door.'

'Think nothing of it. The truth is it gets harder to get a decent night's rest as a body gets older so I'm not blaming you. Now, sit yourself down and I'll get you that cup of tea.'

Pulling out a shaker-style chair from the large pine table, Georgia picked up a pot of marmalade standing with the rest of the jams on the square placemat which had a picture of the Scottish Highlands imprinted on it, and absently read the contents label—her mind preoccupied with the fact that her boss could walk through the door at any minute.

During the night, after he'd left, she'd been kept awake far more by thoughts of him than the thunderous storm. Her lips had ached without cease for the touch of his mouth against hers, for his inviting, addictive taste, and she wondered what would have happened if Moira hadn't knocked at the door when she had. What perturbed Georgia even more was that she would have *welcomed* Keir's kiss instead of repelling it. *What did that mean?*

She'd always avoided becoming involved with

men she worked for and for very good reason. She was responsible for her brother, and that responsibility took precedence over everything else. She had to give Noah the sense of security that had been so devastatingly snatched away from him by the deaths of their parents. And trying to make a living and keep a roof over their heads and not get into debt was hard enough, without making things even harder by getting romantically involved with her boss!

But now it seemed as though all her previous common sense was suddenly coming under serious fire. *It must have been the storm,* Georgia told herself… That was why she'd acted so uncharacteristically. Storms were her Achilles' Heel. Plus the fact that she had truly believed someone had broken into the house. If she hadn't been so jumpy and on edge about those two factors she would never have allowed Keir to even *enter* her room…let alone comfort her and then try to kiss her!

But even as her mind tried desperately to defend her actions, she knew she was only kidding herself. The fact was that she had seriously missed him when he'd been away in New York, and she hadn't been able to wait for him to return. Even though she knew her feelings weren't at all sensible, or even welcome, Georgia couldn't help them. She just hoped that in the cold light of day what had happened wouldn't make things too awkward between them for them to continue to work together. The bottom seemed to drop out of her whole world even at the thought that she might have to leave Glenteign sooner than she'd planned…

'Oh, by the way…the Chief is back from New York, dear. He returned late last night in the middle of that terrible storm! What a homecoming! Come to think of it…it was probably him coming home that woke me up! I don't suppose there's much chance of you having a quiet day today with him back, though, dear. He had his breakfast and then went straight out to see if there was any damage to the gardens. That wind was fierce! No doubt there'll be a few branches thrown about the place—and he was concerned about some rare plants and shrubs that your brother planted too. Anyway, he came back a little while ago, and he's in his study now.'

Swallowing hard, Georgia contemplated the news that Keir was already in his study with mounting trepidation. 'Well, then, I'll have my tea, give Hamish a quick walk, and then join him. By the way, where *is* Hamish?'

Glancing around her, Georgia guiltily realised that she'd forgotten all about the Labrador. *That was how distracted Keir's appearance last night had made her!*

Moira was quick to reassure her. 'Young Lucy came in early, to help me prepare a few meals I've got planned for the next few days. She asked if she might walk Hamish, and I'm afraid I told her yes. Was that all right, dear?'

Georgia rose to her feet again wanting to delay facing Keir until she'd got herself properly together, and saw her last excuse emphatically disappear now that Lucy was walking Hamish.

'Of course it was all right. Be sure and thank her for me when she gets back. Don't worry about the tea, Moira. I'll get one later. I'd better just go and see if the Chief needs anything.'

Keir was surprised to see Georgia enter the room when she did. He hadn't expected her to make such an early-morning appearance—especially when he knew intimately what sort of a disrupted night she'd had. God knew she'd 'disrupted' *his* night too…in more ways than one.

But now, as she carefully closed the heavy oak study door behind her, Keir's examination of her eye-catching figure, and her slim, tanned legs in the knee-length red linen dress, was swift and hungry. Because of that, and because his desire had been frustratingly thwarted last night, his tone was brusque.

'Nobody instructed you to make such an early start. Have you had breakfast?' he demanded.

'I'll get something later.' She frowned as if it was hardly significant. 'Chief Strachan, I—'

'Chief Strachan?' Unable to keep his mockery at bay, Keir twisted his lips grimly. 'Is this how things are going to proceed between us, then? Are you forgetting that I was in your bedroom after midnight, drying your tears because of your terror at the storm, with you dressed in a robe that barely concealed the fact that you were naked underneath it? Under the circumstances, don't you think it a little ridiculous to resort to calling me "Chief Strachan"?'

Georgia's face paled. 'I wasn't deliberately wearing what I was wearing to entice you! And I didn't ask you to come into my room…you just came in anyway!'

'For goodness' sake, don't look so damn offended! What you wear or don't wear to bed is your own business, and I wasn't trying to cast aspersions! Now, what was it you started to tell me?'

Deliberately dismissing her indignation, Keir exhaled on a heavy sigh and got up from his chair. The instant he did, the scent she was wearing caught him with a slide tackle he hadn't seen coming, and it all but brought him to his knees. An innocent and light fragrance had no right to be so powerfully alluring…but on Georgia it clearly was. Not that she needed any artifice to heighten her already immense appeal…

'About last night…'

'Are we going to labour the point all day,

Georgia?' he asked with exasperation. 'Because, strange as it may seem, we do have work to do!'

There was no point in any further discussion about the matter as far as Keir was concerned—even if he *had* left not knowing whether she had a man waiting for her back in London or not. If she had he really didn't want to hear about it, because it would only make this inconvenient attraction he'd developed for her even worse.

Last night he'd realised he was on very dangerous ground. Apart from nearly kissing her, he should never have confessed that he'd missed her as he had. Recalling his mood, he would have perhaps said other things too—things that in the cold light of day he might have regretted.

Whatever mixed-up emotions he was currently feeling, he couldn't afford to lose a perfectly good secretary because of it. Glancing at his appointments diary earlier, it had seemed a certainty that it was going to be another busy week, after having been away, and the last thing he needed or wanted was to have to hunt for another replacement. Yet even though realistically he knew he would have to curb his 'extra curricular' interest in Georgia if he wanted to keep her at Glenteign, he already intuited it would be a near impossible task. There was something about her that kept making him want to let down some of the usual defences he employed around people, and his blood still simmered hotly with the need to make love to her.

In New York he'd had plenty of opportunity to spend time with the beautiful girl he'd promised to get back in touch with when he returned there. Yet each time Keir had deliberately avoided the chances to be more intimate that had been presented. Even his demanding sex drive had not been able to persuade him to take advantage of the situation.

'Look…if you think this can't work any more, and that my being here is causing some kind of problem for you, then I'll simply pack my case, put my things in the car and get out of your hair for good.'

Her chin had lifted with determination and her hazel eyes were flashing. Keir saw that Georgia was quite capable of carrying out her threat. This wasn't how he'd envisaged the start of their morning together at all, but now—because of his frustration and general irritation—a scenario was threatening that he definately did not welcome.

'Oh, no, you don't! You've signed a contract that's binding, and barring illness and acts of God you're obligated to stay here and fulfil it!'

'There's no need to threaten me! I'm fully aware that I made a written promise when I signed my name, and I have always been a person who has kept her word, but—'

'No buts! I need a secretary, and I want you to stay, so let's have no more nonsensical talk about leaving!'

Shaking his head at her as if she was the most irritating woman on the planet and was driving him to complete distraction, Keir strode back to his desk. Staring at the back of his head, Georgia decided that no matter what she said or did there was just no pleasing this man this morning, so she might as well give up trying. She just couldn't work him out. One minute he was acting as if her mere presence was like a thorn in his side, and then last night he'd nearly been going to kiss her!

Just as her heart leapt at the stirring memory, Georgia recalled him asking her if she was in a hurry to leave him. The answer to that was definitely no. She'd only said what she'd said just now because his coldness towards her had upset her. No matter what the Laird of Glenteign thought of her, Georgia couldn't turn her back on him…not yet. Not until it was really time for her to go.

There was obviously a reason he sometimes seemed to shut her out, and the clue lay with his past—she was certain of it. She wanted to help him, so she would stay.

Certain about her decision, she felt her anger dissipate. 'All right,' she agreed. 'I won't talk about leaving any more. We just got off on the wrong foot this morning, that's all. I can see that now.'

She was interlocking her fingers, staring down at them, when she heard the creak of the leather chair that Keir was occupying. When she glanced up again, he had swivelled it round to regard her. Not having entirely finished what she'd been going to say, Georgia sucked in her breath and continued, 'To make things a little easier for both of us, apart from working with you during the day I'll keep out of your way as much as possible at all other times. Then we won't have to make polite conversation with each other when we don't feel like it.'

'That won't be necessary.'

'I don't mind—'

'Didn't you hear what I said? I said that won't be necessary!'

'Oh, for goodness' sake!'

Throwing her hands up in the air in exasperation, Georgia stared at him in disbelief. There was clearly *something* about her that was pressing all the wrong buttons with him this morning—something she just didn't get. Either that, or he was unhappy about something that had happened on his trip.

As soon as the idea had planted itself in her mind, she found she needed to have it confirmed. Georgia didn't want to add to his troubles—all she wanted to do was help alleviate them. Her nature was that she always tried to help.

'Did something go wrong in New York?'

'What?'

'Is that why you seem so on edge?'

Georgia was beginning to wonder if it was a woman that was at the root of his bad mood, and she didn't include herself in spite of Keir's suggestion last night that he'd looked forward to coming back to see her. Had there been a woman Keir liked in New York? A woman he might even be in love with? Had that woman rejected him?

Jealousy vying with fear inside her, Georgia had to work hard to keep her expression impassive.

'Nothing went wrong in New York, Georgia…other than the fact that I didn't really want to be there!'

'But you seemed in such a hurry to go there!' she exclaimed.

'Did I?' His handsome brow creased as though he were perplexed.

'You really are completely impossible!' Georgia accused him, frustrated that she clearly wasn't going to get any answers that made any sense to anything today. Dropping her hands to either side of her shapely hips in the red linen dress, she sighed heavily.

'That aside…perhaps we should both just get down to the business of the day and restore a little peace to the morning? We've had enough storms of one kind or another for a while—wouldn't you agree?'

'Fine! What would you like me to do for you first?' Her temper helplessly simmering, Georgia tossed back her hair and waited for instructions.

Silently surveying him for a moment, she saw a distracting dimple appear at the corner of Keir's disturbing mouth.

'That could take us into a whole new interesting arena if I were deliberately to misconstrue that question.' He grinned. 'Want to ask me again? But perhaps this time with a little less provocative passion?'

CHAPTER SIX

A SHAFT OF SUNLIGHT beamed in from a small side casement window and created a pool of light in the middle of the floor. It lit up the muted reds and golds of an old faded Persian carpet that had been unfolded there a long time ago—possibly even before Keir had been born. Round the edges of that eye-catching pool of light were some of the now superfluous remnants of his family's past.

In one corner were a pair of discarded Tiffany lamps that had once resided in his father's study—the study that now belonged to Keir—and next to them an old oak dresser-cum china cabinet, long empty of any fine display of porcelain and pottery, and now home to a generous coating of dust.

Piled around the room in general haphazard fashion were myriad cardboard boxes, splitting at the seams with books and ornaments and trinkets, and possibly somewhere in amongst all that the beloved chess set that his mother had surprisingly presented to him one Christmas when his father had been away on business. It was a gift that had often been utilised as a means of escape and distraction from James Strachan's sour temper, and its home had nearly always been this attic.

Robbie and Keir would steal away up here as often as they could, to shut the door on their parents' terrible rows, and locked in the strategy of the game would briefly escape the trauma that seemed to underline their childhood. After their mother had died there'd been no more refuge in the attic to play chess.

Both boys had gone to a local public school, as their father had done before them, but they hadn't been allowed to board like most of the other pupils. If they had, Keir sometimes wondered if the bleakness of his home life wouldn't have scarred him quite as badly—but James had seemed to take particular delight in demanding that his sons came home at the end of each school day, just so that he could remain in rigid control of every aspect of their lives and plague them further with his meanness and ill temper.

Made to do various jobs round the house as well as work on the estate, they'd also regularly had to listen to his various rants and small-minded prejudices over the political situation, or his belligerent belief that 'people just don't know their place these days,' and that they should show the gentry more respect. When Keir had invariably started to disagree with his point of view and dared to express his own his father had demonstrated his fury with his fists…

Feeling slightly nauseous at the relentless tide of unwanted memories that washed over him—each one like a stinging cut that had never healed—Keir moved with trepidation into the room and accidentally trod on something hard underfoot. Looking down to see what it was, he picked up a once lovingly painted miniature replica of a nineteenth-century Scottish soldier. For a few moments he scarcely breathed. Then, his palm curling tightly round the small toy, so that the metal edges dug painfully into his flesh, tears stabbed the backs of his eyes like dagger points.

'Robbie…' he murmured fiercely, a thick, merciless ache inside his throat. 'I'm sorry, Robbie…I'm so sorry…'

'Georgia! Are you bringing that coffee?' Keir bellowed.

Turning towards the thickly carpeted staircase, with its almost Gothic carved figures on the newels, Georgia was careful to balance the silver tray she carried as she ascended the stairs. As she went, she took a deep breath in and scowled.

'I wonder whatever happened to good old-fashioned manners?' she grumbled.

Even after the little talk they'd had earlier, her boss had been like a wounded bear all morning, and his mood was showing no sign of improving any time soon. Just as she reached the landing and approached the study door, she saw Keir's tall, broad-shouldered figure impatiently pacing the floor. His dark straight hair, sticking out a little at odd angles, attested to the fact that it had taken the brunt of his impatience. Immediately honing in on her presence, he didn't trouble to conceal his irritation.

'For God's sake, don't hover! Just come inside, will you?' he commanded.

Just about holding onto her own temper at his belligerent mood, Georgia reluctantly crossed the threshold into the study.

'If you remember to say please, I will,' she retorted smartly.

Her glance colliding with his steely blue glare, Georgia's heart bumped indignantly as she carried out his request, her jaw set mutinously to show her displeasure.

So much for restoring some peace to their working morning! The half an hour's breather Keir had taken earlier to—in his own words—'get his head straight' clearly hadn't done much good. Maybe she should suggest he spend some more time on his own?

'I can take the letters into the library and do them there, if you need some privacy for a while?' she offered, thinking that that would probably be the best arrangement. There was a spare computer all set up in there, and it wouldn't be a chore.

She loved the lofty elegant room, with its studious yet inviting ambience, and it was filled to the rafters with books of all kinds. The shelves that contained them were made from oak inlaid with maple, Moira had told her, and some of the books had been in Keir's family for centuries. With its worn but lovely carpets and its big overstuffed sofas and chairs it was a room to sit and dream in, or while away a rainy day in unashamed comfort.

But Georgia saw the flicker of a dissenting muscle in Keir's chiselled cheek and knew that her helpful suggestion had gone down like a lead balloon.

'There's no need for you to go anywhere else. This is where I work, and this is where I expect my secretary to work!'

Standing next to her, he slammed his hand down onto the desk to emphasise his point. The sudden violent movement dislodged the tray Georgia had just placed there, and as he reached out to try and stop it from crashing to the floor the full-to-the-brim silver coffee-pot toppled over, splashing its scalding contents all over his wrist.

'Arrgh! Damn!'

Georgia acted immediately.

'Let's get you to a bathroom. We'll go to the one

across the hall.' Already with her hand at his back, she started to push him towards the door.

'I don't bloody believe this!' he muttered furiously.

Examining his shocked face, Georgia led him into the marble-tiled bathroom and hurriedly turned the cold tap full on. As the water gushed out from the faucet she held his arm beneath it, watching it soak into the coffee stained sleeve covering his forearm. She wouldn't be attempting to peel back the material until she was certain that no skin would come away with it.

'We need to do this for at least ten minutes,' she told him, her heart racing fast at what had happened. 'Thank God the coffee wasn't quite boiling hot… By the time I'd brought it from the kitchen and came up the stairs it would have cooled down considerably. I don't think you'll need to go to hospital, but it will probably sting like crazy for a few hours or more. Are you okay?'

Acting purely on impulse, she pushed back a lock of his midnight-dark hair. But seeing him flinch, she wondered if she had taken a liberty she shouldn't have.

'I'm fine.' His breath exhaled on a ragged sigh, Keir turned to glance sideways at Georgia, a surprising lift at one corner of his mouth. 'I didn't know you were a trained nurse in one of your previous incarnations,' he commented wryly.

'I did some first-aid training with the St John's Ambulance organisation. When you're left to raise a fourteen-year old boy all on your own, you need to know some basic first-aid skills, let me tell you!'

'Ouch!' He blanched as Georgia gently moved his arm, to make sure the water was reaching the entire area where the coffee had been spilt. 'I'm lucky that you were around and knew what to do,' he remarked.

It struck Keir then that he felt total confidence in Georgia's healing skills. She was capable and firm when she needed to be, and yet exceedingly gentle too. As her calm voice washed over him and her soft skin inevitably came into contact with his, where she held his hand and guided his forearm beneath the splashing water, he was aware that even though he was in considerable pain he very much *liked* this sudden enforced closeness with Georgia.

Moira Guthrie put her head round the door just then, her flushed round face bearing rosy evidence that she'd rushed up the stairs.

'What on earth has happened?' she asked breathlessly, coming into the room. 'I was in the hall and I heard you cry out. Oh, good gracious! Was it the hot coffee, lassie?'

As she saw that Georgia had clearly taken charge, and knew what she was doing, some of the anxiety drained out of the housekeeper's face.

'It spilled across his wrist. Just a little longer,' Georgia told Keir, when she saw him flinch again in pain. 'Believe me this will help. Moira, do you think you could find me a clean, dry dressing? And if you wouldn't mind going into my bedroom and getting my handbag? I've got some arnica in there, which is good for shock. We'll wait here.'

'Stupid bloody thing to happen!' His expression fierce for a moment, Keir shook his head from side to side as if in disbelief.

'I've often found that when I'm angry I end up hurting myself somehow,' Georgia shared with him gently, not wanting to inflame his temper any further, but needing to make what she hoped was a helpful observation. 'Perhaps you need to find a safer way to release the anger you're holding on to and let it go?'

'No doubt you're right.'

He reflected on his reluctant yet compelling visit to the attic earlier—the first in the nine months since he'd been back at Glenteign. He'd been searching for something... exactly what he didn't know...but something that might give him some clue as to how he was going to overcome this great weight of sorrow and pain in his heart. But Keir had not left that room of memories feeling much forgiveness or any closure in his heart about his past. Instead, rage had welled up inside him afresh at what he and Robbie had endured, and the indelible scars it had left him with.

He was only beginning to realise now, after suffering this stupid accident, how dangerous it was to let that rage dominate his emotions. Georgia—in her surprising wisdom—was absolutely correct with her sage advice. Except that Keir didn't know how he could begin to 'safely' release the rage and hurt he felt inside. Since he'd been back at Glenteign he'd almost felt like a prisoner there, locked inside his painful memories, with reminders at every turn, instead of a man in charge of his own destiny. He knew that such a debilitating state of affairs could not go on…

'But there are some things that are almost too damn hard to do and, I can't help the way I feel,' he continued, his mouth a thin, bitter line. 'What? You're not going to tell me I should try harder?'

There was something so bleak in his riveting blue gaze as he trained it directly on Georgia's face that her heart constricted in pain. She tore her glance from his with difficulty, and focused once more on the running water splashing onto his arm.

'I wouldn't presume to tell you what to do. I think you just need to try and stay calm. It won't help the pain if you get yourself more agitated…no matter whether you're hurting inside or out.'

Minutes later, Moira appeared with a small first aid kit, from which Georgia selected a dressing of the appropriate size. She instructed Keir to sit down in the cane chair next to the bath so that she could apply it to his arm. Thankfully, she was able to peel back the soaked material without any detrimental effect to his scalded skin. The wound looked red and angry, but she could already tell that in a week to ten days' time it would heal nicely, without even leaving a scar.

Relief ebbed through her in a thankful wave and, tipping out an arnica tablet from the packet she had taken from her handbag, she gave it to Keir. 'Put this on the end of your tongue and let it dissolve. It will help with the shock. I'm just going to put this dressing on for you, and then you should go and put your feet up for a while. Perhaps you could lie on one of the big sofas in the library? They're nice and comfy. Then I'll bring you up a cup of hot, sweet tea.'

'Oh I can do that for the Chief, lassie! I'll find some of his favourite biscuits too.'

Glad to have something else to do other than stand by and watch Georgia put Keir's dressing on, Moira bustled out of the room again.

Finishing her task, Georgia sat back on the edge of the bath and smiled. 'I think you'll live to fight another day!'

'Thanks to you.' Grimly examining the stark white dressing covering a large area of his forearm, Keir quickly moved his gaze to look at Georgia instead. 'My own private nurse as well as my very efficient secretary… Does your after-care extend to tucking me into bed tonight, I wonder?'

'Definitely not!' Although her retort was smart, Georgia sensed a wave of heat suffuse her cheeks.

'Pity.'

There was the semblance of a rueful smile about his lips, but his piercing blue eyes could not disguise his longing.

Trying to convince herself that it must simply be the aftermath of shock, or the surge of adrenaline that came with it, Georgia regarded his hard handsome face with renewed concern. With its sculpted lean angles and the firm cleft in the centre of his rather arrogant chin, there was something about it that was so compelling that she was filled with the strongest, almost irresistible desire to touch him. Not just with the gentle ministrations of a healer either. But with the almost overwhelmingly demanding need of a woman who knew herself to be dangerously beguiled by him…

'You really should go and lie down for a while!' she exclaimed, jumping up from the edge of the bath. 'We have to be careful that shock doesn't set in. You can be quite ill otherwise. Shall I help you into the library?'

It was quite remarkable to Keir that he could be in so much pain from his scald and yet so imbued with desire for the woman who had tended him that he could scarcely think straight! So much so that he didn't want to go and lie down alone. If Georgia came with him, then that would be quite a different matter entirely…

Yet even as the thought grew into the most compelling demand, Keir already guessed that she would refuse him. She would no doubt have a raft of principles behind her refusal too. Number one being that he had hired her as his temporary secretary, and that was the only obligation she'd come to Glenteign to fulfil… Not to alleviate any carnal desire her boss might have!

She was clearly a woman of integrity, and he couldn't fault her for that—even though it didn't help his case right now one little bit.

'I don't need your help to walk down the corridor into the library, dammit!' he replied irritably. 'I've scalded my arm, not broken my leg!'

As he got up and went through the door, Georgia stared at him in astonished disbelief. 'Well, I'm so happy to see that your accident hasn't curtailed in any way your ability to be as cantankerous and belligerent as ever!' she declared out loud to his back.

Turning at this daring attempt not to be browbeaten by his temper, Keir felt his blood throb with renewed heat as he confronted her beautiful indignant face. Driven to act by purely primal instinct—he crossed the floor in one fluid stride and with his uninjured arm yanked her hard against his chest.

'This has been coming for a long time,' he ground out, just before he covered her mouth passionately with his own.

The hard yet compelling mouth that took command of her lips was bordering on the brutal with its untamed, ravenous demand. But as the velvet magic of Keir's hot silken tongue ruthlessly seduced her, causing an explosion of untrammelled sensation throughout her body, Georgia felt an answering cry of profound need ring out in her heart. To feel such raw physical need was a revelation to her. She'd suppressed so much that to have those potentially dangerous feelings blown apart now by this man's expert, ruthless kiss, was deeply shocking and yet wildly liberating at the same time.

She had been guarded all her life. Always, always she had thought of her brother's welfare first, and of how his upbringing might be jeopardised should she allow herself to fall in love and commit her future to someone else. What if the man she fell in love with could not find it in his heart to be kind to Noah? What if he didn't understand the closeness between brother and sister and sought to end or destroy it?

These questions had always loomed large whenever she'd nursed fantasies about meeting someone special…someone she wanted to spend the rest of her life with.

Now, the heated addictive pressure on her mouth

started to ease, degree by tormenting degree, and Keir's arm slackened a little on her waist. To Georgia's surprise his kiss became gentler, kinder—more seductive even—and her chest was tight with emotion and yearning. When he finally withdrew his lips from hers, she saw such raw, unfettered need reflected there in his amazing blue eyes that it made her feel almost faint with longing.

'I think I *will* go and lie down on one of the sofas in the library,' he teased gently, his nostrils flaring a little. 'I seem to have acquired a sudden added complication in that my blood pressure has just gone sky-high. What remedies do you have for bringing it down again, Nurse?'

Now it was Keir's turn to sweep back a lock of hair from Georgia's brow, and the tender way he did it elicited such joy inside her that it made her light-headed. Perhaps she ought to be furious with him for taking such a liberty as to kiss her so uninhibitedly and brazenly. But of all the emotions that were sweeping through her right then, fury did not feature at all.

Clearing her throat with difficulty, her lips still throbbing from his hungry, fiery kisses as though they would never cease to ache, Georgia wondered if her compliance showed in her eyes. 'Rest,' she advised softly, her hazel glance reflecting myriad greens and golds. 'Plenty of rest. I'll tell Moira to take your tea into the library.'

'Thank you.' Smiling ruefully at having to leave her, Keir finally set Georgia free with a light brush of his hand against her cheek.

His touch felt as if it burned her. She watched him move towards the door as if she were in a trance.

'I will see you later,' he promised. And leaving her, he made his way down the hall to the library…

CHAPTER SEVEN

HE'D BEEN DEEP in the throes of the most erotic dream he'd ever had… Now, stirring to wakefulness on one of the old overstuffed sofas in the library, his brow damp with perspiration and the very devil of a searing pain in his arm, Keir sat up feeling dazed, and rubbed his hand round his studded jaw.

It was hard to tell which pain was worse… The scald he'd acquired from the hot coffee, or the strong throbbing ache in the region of his groin… The dream had been so damn real that Keir could swear he'd been making uninhibited passionate love to one dark-haired, hazel-eyed sorceress who, in turn, had done things to him that would make a grown man sink down onto his knees and give thanks that he had been incarnated as a male in this lifetime…

'Bloody hell!' He exclaimed out loud. Not because he shouldn't be nursing such lascivious thoughts about his temporary secretary, but because she wasn't there with him to carry out his fantasy for *real*...

Keir reflected that now he had enforced an intimacy between himself and Georgia that there was probably no turning back. Perhaps it had been reckless of him, but even *his* infamous iron will could not resist the pure temptation that was Noah Cameron's shapely, beguiling, sister. Things had really started to get out of hand when she'd pushed back that lock of hair from his brow. Her touch had been so exquisite, so infinitely kind, that Keir had been undone by it. No one had ever touched him in such a tender, almost *loving* way...

He froze at how dangerously his emotions seemed to be unravelling. *What the hell was he thinking of?* Georgia Cameron fascinated him, and he definitely admired her as a person—how could he not when she had so many amazing qualities?—but right now he had only one goal in mind as far as she was concerned, and that was to simply seduce her. Anything beyond that—especially anything remotely appertaining to emotional need—was simply a fantasy on Keir's part, no doubt brought about by what had just happened to him.

Yet, even if that most basic physical need were fulfilled, would he find it that easy to let her go? He wanted more from this woman than mere sex—although he hesitated to confirm in his own mind what that something 'more' was.

He'd always found it difficult to relate to the concept or even the possibility of needing a deeper response from anyone. He even kept his platonic friendships as uncomplicated and commitment-free as possible. There was a deeply held belief inside him that somehow the taint of his unhappy past would ultimately end up destroying those friendships, and so inevitably he did not allow anyone to get too close to him. There were very few, if any among his acquaintances, who could really say that they knew him.

Now, glancing down at his watch, Keir experienced mild shock when he saw the time. Had he really slept most of the afternoon away? As he made himself stand, he tried to shake off the slightly unreal and stuffy feeling in his head that made him feel as if he'd been drugged. He was thirsty, he was hungry, and his burn throbbed like merry hell! Had anybody in the household come to check on him whilst he'd been sleeping?

As he reached the door and wrenched it open with a disgruntled frown, Keir knew full well the person he'd hoped would have undertaken that task was Georgia.

Georgia had set off walking about half an hour before dinner, to try and get her head straight. She'd hardly had any peace since Keir had kissed her, and now her feelings were in absolute turmoil.

Walking in nature usually provided a release from such inner turmoil, she'd found, and so she'd resorted to the one thing that might help her. But now she realised that the inevitable spell of the mountains and lochs had weaved their magic too potently around her senses, and the distance she'd inadvertently covered because of her enchantment was too great to allow her to get back to Glenteign in time to sit down to the evening meal with everyone else.

Damn!

Even Hamish looked up at her with reproach in his big dark eyes, his great tongue lolling as he panted hard at his exertion. Dropping down onto her haunches, Georgia affectionately stroked back the champagne coloured fur on his head and sighed heavily.

'I'm sorry, Hamish! I just lost track of time. Never mind—you'll have your dinner as soon as we get back to Glenteign, I promise. We'd better get our skates on, though, because it looks like it might rain again!'

Glancing up at the darkening grey clouds that were gathering so threateningly in the previously flawless blue sky, Georgia sensed sudden fear knife through her. The last thing in the world she wanted to do was to be caught out in a storm to equal the one they'd had last night! It was one thing being inside, watching it safely from a bedroom window, but quite another witnessing the full brunt of its elemental passion outside in the open!

Falling into a jog, she nervously increased her pace as a sudden spot of rain splashed onto her face…

'Where the *hell* has she got to?'

The harshly expressed question did not fail to conceal the underlying anxiety in Keir's voice as he paced to one of the huge dining room windows and glanced out.

Watching his stiff back in the dark cashmere sweater, and feeling the tension in him transmit itself to the other members of staff in the room, Moira silently admitted to her own concerns about the young secretary since she'd failed to turn up for dinner. She'd seen her go out with Hamish shortly after she'd finished work—and she hoped the girl had not gone and got herself lost. It was easy to do if a person didn't know their way well round these parts. The mountainous region around Glenteign was so vast that even an experienced guide could easily make a wrong turn. Now the Chief's obvious anxiety over Georgia's absence was putting her on edge as well. Especially as outside the rain had started to pour as though it would never cease, and they'd all heard that angry rumble of thunder vent its spleen above them only moments ago.

'Someone had better go and find her.'

Standing up from the dining table in the smaller, more intimate dining room where they'd just had their meal, Moira glanced across the polished maple-wood table at one of the young gardeners employed on the estate—a lad who worked alongside his father, who was head gardener there. Both men knew the area well.

'Euan, will you go? The lassie told me she was a bit nervous of storms, and she might get disoriented trying to find her way back in the rain.'

'*I'll* go.' Already at the door, and pulling it wide, Keir turned briefly to glance at the others round the table. 'She's probably not far away.'

'Get a mackintosh from the mudroom before you go, Chief. You don't want to be getting soaked to the skin or get that dressing all wet after your accident today!'

On her feet as she started collecting up the plates to take them into the kitchen, Moira didn't hesitate to advise him.

Without a word, Keir turned and went out.

Just as he reached the bottom of the concrete steps that led down onto the gravel drive, he saw a blur of vivid colour in the distance and realised that it was Georgia, jogging towards the house, Hamish slightly ahead of her. The relief that washed through him could not be measured.

But even as he sensed the tension ease out of his shoulders a scissor-flash of lightning slashed through the sky with an ear-splitting crack, and Keir saw Georgia pause to look up. She started to run again, but a moment later she seemed to trip and pitch forward in the middle of the glistening emerald lawn. Immediately the faithful Labrador ran back to be with her.

Without another thought, Keir started to run towards her. The driving rain pummelled at his clothing where he hadn't bothered to do up the waterproof he'd quickly donned on the way out. When he reached her, Georgia was starting to struggle to her feet, her red linen dress covered in loose wet grass and splashes of mud. Her long dark hair was tangled, and almost plastered to her shocked face, and her hazel eyes couldn't contain their fear.

'What have you done to yourself?' he demanded, concern making his tone gruffly impatient. 'You haven't hurt your ankle?'

'I just slipped on the wet grass,' she replied, shivering. 'I'm all right…really.'

She might not be hurt physically, but Keir easily detected that the lightning strike and the thunder had shaken her up badly. Giving no thought to his own injured arm, he swept her up against his chest and started to hurry with her towards the house.

'You don't have to carry me!' Georgia protested,

shocked. 'Keir, I'm quite capable of walking… really!'

But he carried her just the same, his dark face stoic and determined as he held her, his racing heart attesting to the maelstrom of emotion that was going on inside him at being able to hold her so close, uncaring that her own soaked clothing was making his even wetter.

By the time they reached the house and Keir had ordered the faithful Labrador to go round to the back door Moira was at the front, her face amply illustrating her anxiety and relief.

'What happened, lassie? Are you hurt?' The kindly housekeeper reached out to help her from Keir's arms, but the Laird's almost warning glare made her drop them down by her sides again immediately.

'I'm not hurt. I'm fine—honestly… I told Keir I was fine! I simply slipped on the wet grass because I was hurrying to get out of the storm, that's all.' Her teeth chattering, but on her feet once more, Georgia glanced at the other woman with what she hoped was a reassuring smile. 'Can I ask you if you'd mind seeing to Hamish? He's gone round to the back door. I just need to get out of these wet clothes and go and get a hot shower.'

'Of course I will, my dear! You go and get yourself dry before you catch your death!'

'Thanks…I appreciate it.'

Withdrawing from them, hating being the centre of attention, Georgia stepped quickly away from the protection of Keir's warm, hard body to cross the chequered entrance hall and start ascending the grand winding staircase.

'I've put your dinner in the oven to keep warm,' Moira called up behind her. 'You come down and have it when you're ready.'

Even though the spray from the shower had been wonderfully reassuring and hot, Georgia sat in her towelling robe on the edge of the quaintly old-fashioned brass bed and sensed her body shiver as though it might never stop.

What had possessed Keir to pick her up and carry her like that? As though he wanted to put himself between her and harm? The threatened storm might have secretly terrified her, but she was far more scared of the torrent of wild feelings that gripped her whenever he came near.

Staring at the wall, she recalled the look of surprise on Moira's face when she'd reached out to help her and Keir had somehow dissuaded her with just a single determined glance. Things were beginning to get complicated, she realised. As if some unstoppable force was having its way and there was nothing she could do about it… Unless, of course, she decided to leave…

Her heart racing, Georgia glanced across at the casement windows of her room, at the rain that was still rattling the little square panes. A disconcerting emptiness and a yearning that she didn't want to name gnawed at her, and the depth and power of the sensation almost drove her to tears.

'Georgia? Is everything all right?'

At first she was disorientated, not knowing who spoke, then in almost the same instant she realised that the extraordinarily compelling voice could only belong to Keir. Standing up to go to the door, she tidied the front of her robe, making sure she was adequately covered, at the same time cursing silently that she hadn't dressed straight away—because once again she was at an embarrassing disadvantage.

But there was no need to open the door, was there? Georgia could merely assure him that she was fine and he would quickly go away again.

'Yes…everything's okay. I'll be down shortly. I'm just—I'm just getting dressed.'

'Open the door, will you? I want to see you.'

So much for *that* plan! Feeling her breath grow tight inside her chest, she briefly wiped her palms down the sides of her robe before reaching for the door catch.

'What is it?'

Her aim had been to simply open the door just a little—enough for him to see for himself that she was fine—and Georgia was unprepared for that decision being immediately taken out of her hands.

He swept decisively through the opening, then shut the door firmly behind him, and the sheer physicality of the man simply overwhelmed her as she found herself staring up into his starkly handsome face, his searing blue eyes burning her with the force of intensity she saw glimmering there. Helplessly suspended in the tension of the moment, her limbs feeling peculiarly as though they no longer belonged to her, Georgia went very still. Her heart continued to beat but she didn't know how…

Before so much as another word or even a breath had left her lips, she felt herself seized by Keir's strong muscular arms and impelled almost roughly up against his chest.

'I only needed a temporary secretary,' he commented, almost with disdain, as he glared down into her shocked face. 'And now I can't even *think* about work with you around distracting me! Just what the hell am I supposed to do about you, Georgia?'

CHAPTER EIGHT

HIS MOUTH WAS on hers before she could utter a word, and suddenly their breath was one breath. His kisses tasted of the Glens, with their intoxicating pure fresh air, and almost made her high. His body against hers was like tempered steel, hard and honed, with an almost desperate undercurrent of need that wouldn't be constrained.

He'd demanded to know what he was supposed to do about her, and Georgia knew the question was equally true for her. *What was she supposed to do about her growing feelings for him?* The spellbinding magnetism that was created whenever they were near each other now indubitably held sway. It was as she'd observed…an unstoppable force that knew no bounds.

Helping Keir earlier, when he'd scalded himself with the coffee, Georgia had automatically acted to do what she could—but, as well as hopefully alleviating his agony, she couldn't deny the intense pleasure she'd received at being able to touch him without question.

Now her gaze cleaved to his resolute jaw as he slid one arm beneath her knees and the other behind her back, then carried her across the carpeted floor to the sturdy, old-fashioned brass bed.

'Be careful of your wound!' she pleaded urgently, her voice almost breaking.

A rueful smile touched the corners of his mouth as he carefully laid her down on the bed. '*What* wound?' he joked. 'I hardly feel any pain any more. The only ache that's disturbing me now is my wanting you, Georgia... You know that, don't you?'

Her heart skipped at his very serious concentrated expression. 'I know that... But do you—do you have something to...' She couldn't help it. Her face flamed because she'd had to ask him the question. A question she'd never asked another man before in her life...

Wordlessly he removed a small packet from his jeans pocket. He laid it down on top of the small oak cabinet beside the bed, next to the suspense novel she'd brought from home to read. Then, stripping off his shirt, he held her gaze with his piercing blue eyes as a fierce shining star commanded and held the blackness of the night.

Georgia wanted Keir so badly that if a spaceship

had materialised in the room during those electrifying moments, she wouldn't have noticed. Her eyes ate him up as she watched him undress. The more he revealed of himself, the more her heart pounded with ferocious joy. Confronted with his breathtaking masculinity, registering the impact of his strong, fit physique, she felt her senses utterly enraptured by him. Her gaze lit too on the stark white dressing on his arm, and she silently commiserated anew with the pain he must have endured.

Her breath was released on a soft onrush of air as he came to her, unfastening the tie of her robe with hands that were sure and strong, then peeling the garment easily from her body. Before he could say anything Georgia lifted her arms and wrapped them around his neck.

Hearing the ragged sigh that broke free from his lips at the contact with her bare soft skin, she whispered, 'I know we shouldn't be doing this…but I don't want to stop.'

'If it's what we both want, then there's no reason to stop… Have you never given into pure naked desire before, Georgia?'

She didn't want to answer that question lest it incriminate her. She was walking a tightrope of tension, despite the heady rush of adrenalin and need pulsing through her body, but she did not intend to let fear or doubt rule the day. *It would be all right…*

It *had* to be all right. For once in her life she was thinking of no one else's needs but her own.

The sudden sensation of his firm warm silky skin next to hers made Georgia's insides tighten with longing, but instead of fearing this new territory she was venturing into she found herself welcoming it. Her mouth slipped over his with unselfconscious eagerness, tasting moisture, heat and demand in one divinely erotic press, and her body knew no dissent only a deeply carnal hunger when he tipped her back onto the bed and covered her nakedness with his.

Readily allowing Keir's hands to explore her, Georgia heard her own breathless sighs drown out the steady repetitive hush of the rain that accompanied them. His mouth languorously tasted her velvet-tipped breasts—taking his time, giving her pleasure and receiving it, sucking and caressing them until her whole being was consumed with fierce tingles of the most erotic joy. Was this how a flower felt…opening for the first time to the miracle of rain…the caress of sunlight? As if its very being was created anew by that seductive, addictive touch? Even Georgia's quite considerable imagination had not prepared her for the river of hot sweet delight that poured through her veins at Keir's touch.

Her hand brushed against his strong, hot erection with curiosity and lust, and she heard his almost painful groan in response. Inside, answering heat drenched her. Without another word he moved her hand away, and started to unwrap the little foil package he'd left on the bedside cabinet. When he'd sheathed himself in the contents, he started to slowly press himself inside her. Holding on to the broad, muscular slopes of his shoulders, Georgia stared into Keir's eyes and felt as if she was being consumed by electric blue fire so intense was the gaze that commanded hers.

Silently she told herself to relax. She knew all she had to do was surrender to the powerful melting tide that was softening her hips and making her breasts throb in an agony of desire. *She'd been made for this...* Any momentary hurt would quickly pass, and then all she would know was the pleasure...

When he finally penetrated her all the way, Georgia was unable to hold back her cry of pain. Keir's surprised glance searched her face with stunned enquiry, and his hard jaw momentarily tightened.

Moving her hand behind his head, Georgia leaned up towards him and pulled his face down to hers. In less than a moment he was kissing her with renewed passion, her pain forgotten, his demanding thrusts inside her body growing deeper and harder, enforcing a rhythm between them that built with urgency at each passing second.

Just before she sensed his whole body tense and

then finally let go, the muscles in the tops of his arms bunching like iron as she held on to them, Georgia rode the sweetly fierce tide that swept her up in its powerful current and felt as if she was flying. Ripples of intoxicating delight ebbed through her body, again and again and again. A strange kind of calm stole over her in its dizzying aftermath. Dazed, she accepted Keir's final powerful claim on her body, and then he stilled and laid his head against her chest. She sensed him shudder violently with his own release. She shut her eyes in silent awe…

What had he done? His heart feeling like a bass drum, pounding out its rhythm inside his chest, Keir rolled away from Georgia and lay on his back, breathing hard. *Good God!* He'd never in a million years anticipated such an unbelievable surprise. As soon as she'd cried out he'd known that this was her first time…her *first!* Astonishingly Georgia Cameron, until a few minutes ago, had been a virgin. And Keir had accepted the gift of her innocence with scant hesitation—choosing to ignore the gravity of the deed to achieve his own lustful satisfaction.

He knew why. Lately, instead of the common sense he could usually summon so easily to his aid, he'd let down his guard and allowed himself to be driven by emotions and feelings as far as this woman was concerned. It was a definite first.

Now, as he turned to regard her, the dark silk skeins of her hair tousled on the pillow behind her, Keir saw that Georgia's eyes were curiously closed. Had she retreated into her own private world perhaps to make her peace with what had happened between them? He only hoped that she wasn't regretting it. What if she'd secretly had some idea of saving her virginity for the love of her life? A flicker of the most profound unease assaulted his insides at the thought. Then he reminded himself that she hadn't repelled him at any point. She'd been as eager as he had for them to make love…

Reaching out, he captured one of the shining soft brown curls that lay coiled against her shoulder and saw her start. Her hazel eyes opened in surprise and studied him, glazed with the hazy softness of love-making. Her words, nonetheless, belied what had just taken place between them. 'Moira will be wondering where on earth I've got to. She was expecting me down for my dinner,' she said calmly.

It was a ruse. Instinctively Keir knew that she was delaying the inevitable moment when they would have to discuss the momentous event that had just taken place between them, and he sensed her anxiety.

'You should have told me,' he said quietly, withdrawing his hand.

'Should I?' Her voice faltered a little and she bit her lip. 'Would it have stopped you making love to me if you'd known?'

'I'm not saying that. But you should have mentioned it at least!'

'Why? Do you have something against virgins?' she asked mockingly, her expression unable to mask her hurt. 'Don't most men think we're such a *prize?* Admittedly, twenty-eight-year-old virgins are probably fairly thin on the ground, but sometimes it's good to break the mould…don't you think?'

Before he could stop her, she'd grabbed the linen sheet, wrapped it round her naked form, and moved away across the room to the window. Presenting her back to him, Georgia gazed out at the teeming rain as though it hypnotised her.

Confused and angry at her blasé attitude, Keir collected his boxers and jeans and hurriedly pulled them on over his own nakedness. Barefoot, he strode across the luxuriously thick carpet to join her. Before she could say anything, he spun her round and forced her to look at him.

'Why?' he asked her, his gaze hard.

'Why what? Look…you're really making a mountain out of a molehill, you know!'

At Keir's answering glower, Georgia shrugged.

'All right then. You want to know why I stayed a virgin up until now?' There was a small but discernible quiver of her prettily shaped top lip. 'After taking care of Noah, earning my living has always had to be the top priority in my life. I simply didn't have the time or the energy to devote to an intimate relationship.'

'Other people manage.' Keir was striving to understand her.

'Well…other people have different situations and priorities. Since my parents died, mine has been taking responsibility for Noah, making sure that the mortgage and the bills are paid and that we have enough to eat.'

'After your parents died, didn't you and Noah inherit the family home?'

'We did…but it wasn't paid for. We only inherited the mortgage.'

It seemed to Keir as if her beautiful green-gold eyes clouded over with sadness for a moment.

'My father got into trouble with his business and accumulated quite a bit of debt before he died…that's why. I had to work hard to help pay that off too.' She shrugged, clearly uncomfortable at having been made to reveal such a precarious situation.

Now that he knew her reason for staying a virgin for so long, Keir was stunned. She'd sacrificed a life and a relationship of her own for her brother, as well as taking on her parents' debts. Rarely, if ever, had Keir encountered such selfless love and devotion. Absently he laid his hand on his flat, lean stomach and rubbed it, a myriad of conflicting emotions flooding through him at that moment.

'And just how long did you intend to carry on putting Noah's needs before your own, Georgia?' he gently enquired.

'It's not a question of—'

'How long?' Keir insisted.

'I didn't have any finite date in mind! When someone is depending on you, you just get on with things! I know he's a man now, and the business is starting to take off, but I suppose I just got so used to doing what I was doing that it became a habit not to think about a—a relationship with someone.'

She held the sheet tightly in front of her breasts, as though to protect herself.

And even though he clearly saw that she was vulnerable right then, Keir almost wanted to shake her. He could scarcely believe that she'd been willing to put her brother's welfare above her own for so long. When he thought of his tense relationship with his own brother—a factor that maybe he should have been more diligent in trying to improve—Keir silently confessed to feeling slightly ashamed.

'But you must have dated men, surely? Didn't you ever let anybody get close?'

'I went out on a couple of dates, but I never encouraged the men concerned to take things further,' she replied flatly, pushing her fingers through her tumbled locks. 'I was always worried that the energy it would take to commit to a relationship might encroach on what I had to do to survive.'

'But this is your *life* we're talking about, Georgia!'

Yes, it *was* her life and hearing Keir say the words out loud made her realise that it was about time she started to consider what she really wanted for herself. The momentous event that had just occurred had awakened her as thoroughly as though she'd been asleep for the past twenty-eight years—and finally woken up to reality. Transported to another realm by the hot tide of lust and urgent carnal demand that had gripped her body so emphatically in Keir's arms, Georgia had at last discovered her own sensual nature. And, more profoundly, she'd discovered that she wanted to be loved by a man. She didn't want to spend the rest of her life alone.

Her parents' death had cost her dear in more ways than one. She'd expended so much time, energy and devotion on taking care of Noah and keeping their family home together that she'd honestly doubted she was capable of committing herself totally to a relationship—but now a real flicker of hope was burning inside her, and she didn't want to let that flame of hope go out.

'I'm quite aware that it's my life… And if you imagine that I don't have hopes and dreams of my own then you're wrong—because I do!'

Tears were horrendously close, boiling up behind her lids, while her throat felt as if she'd swallowed razorblades and hot water.

'Noah is a lucky man to have such a devoted sister. You're an amazing woman, Georgia…and the man that you eventually end up with will be a very lucky man too.' His expression was unrelenting in its intensity, and Keir knew he meant every word of that compliment. Even if the idea of her ending up with someone else seemed to trigger an avalanche of hurt inside him.

'And what about—?' She seemed to hesitate to pursue her question. 'What about what just happened between us?'

God, she was so innocent! Keir's heart seemed to stall inside his chest at the realisation.

'It was probably inevitable! You can't suppress your own needs for ever…eventually something has to give!'

'So…'

He saw her absorb what he'd said with what seemed like distress. 'What you're saying is I could have gone to bed with anybody? It just happened to be you?'

'No! I'm not saying that at all! It's obvious that we're more than a little attracted to each other, and you are a very desirable woman. Good God! I almost knocked your door down to get you into bed—have you forgotten that?'

It was a cast-iron certainty that Keir hadn't! Even now his body ached with an almost unholy ache to be inside her again. Touching Georgia, making love to her, drowning his senses in the hypnotic intoxication of her body's sweet perfume, had brought him the most indescribable delight. Nothing he'd experienced in a long time could compare with it. And then there was the fact that he was her *first.* He would always be the keeper of that precious gift she had given him, and he couldn't deny the surge of jealousy that all but cut a painful swathe through his insides at the thought that she might ever make love with someone else.

Now, seeing her shoulders drop a little, Keir had to own the surprising feelings of protectiveness and warmth towards her that were assailing him.

'Georgia? Did you hear what I said?'

'Yes…I heard. I'd better get dressed. Moira will be—'

'How can you think of food at a time like this?' Unable to conceal the need that had been growing inside him even as they were talking, Keir knew his desire must be written all over his face as he stared down into Georgia's beautiful startled eyes.

'I didn't get to eat my dinner, remember?'

'Come back to bed.' He hooked his finger in the front of the linen sheet she'd wrapped round herself, at the place between her breasts, and tugged until the two ends came apart and the material slithered down her naked body.

'Keir! We can't. What will—what will everyone think if we don't go downstairs again?'

Keir didn't need to see the sudden delightful contraction of her soft pink nipples to know that she was as turned on by the idea as he was…

'To hell with what anybody else thinks! They don't even know that we're together. I told Moira that I had some work to do. If anybody knocks at your door, then you can just call out that you're tired and having an early night. Later, when the rest of the house is asleep, I'll take you downstairs to the kitchen and we'll raid the fridge together!'

Secretly delighted by this previously unseen playful side to his nature, nonetheless Georgia was doubtful. 'I can't let you do that.' She tried to tug back the hand he had captured.

'What?' His expression was deeply amused. 'Raid my own fridge?'

'I didn't mean that. I came here to work for you, remember? I know it's too late to undo what's just happened, but we shouldn't be making things even more complicated by repeating it!'

'Do you regret the fact that we made love?' he demanded, his vivid blue eyes attesting to his sudden doubt. 'Would you have preferred it if the man you gave your virginity to was the man you were in love with?'

Keir's words were akin to setting off a small earthquake inside her, and Georgia almost swayed. What would he say if he discovered that she *had* given her virginity to the man she was in love with? Finally admitting tho truth to herself, she felt the realisation rock her very soul to its foundations.

'I don't regret it at all!' she exclaimed. 'And I had no grand plan about saving myself for anyone! I've already told you why things were the way they were. I'm simply trying to be sensible about this. I know it's a bit like putting the cart before the horse, but we have to work together until your own secretary returns and I don't want to ruin things.'

'Nothing will be ruined,' he insisted, impelling her forcibly into his arms. 'We're both adults, aren't we? We'll just carry on as normal and nobody else has to know anything unless you want them to.'

Even as he said the words Georgia felt uneasy. What if Keir's housekeeper found out? Or one of the other members of staff? What if they thought that she was taking advantage of her situation working for the Laird? She would hate any of them to imagine for even one second that she was some self-seeking unprincipled opportunist! *And she wasn't convinced by Keir's statement that nothing would be ruined.* He had no idea that she had realized she was already in love with him, and that just made the situation even more precarious!

'I really think that we should put the brakes on here.'

Easing herself out of his arms and stooping to pick up the sheet again, Georgia held it to her front. Inside her chest, her heart thrummed with regret and pain that she couldn't easily curtail her instinct to be sensible and allow Keir to take her back to bed again. Her only consolation was that given time he might thank her for behaving more rationally.

'Okay. I can see that you've made up your mind about this. Even though I would do a hell of a lot to persuade you differently.' Touching his knuckles tenderly to her cheek, Keir turned away from her with an audible sigh.

Wishing she could just relent and tell him she'd changed her mind, Georgia watched him go over to the bed, pick up his shirt, then leave the room without saying even one more word…

CHAPTER NINE

IN SEARCH OF some strong black coffee the next morning to chase the 'fog' from his brain because he'd hardly slept the night before for thinking, Keir strode into the large country-house kitchen only to find Georgia already there.

She was wearing a long tunic-style lilac shirt over matching loose trousers. Nonetheless, the silken cloth lovingly outlined her shapely hips and *derrière* as she reached up to the old-fashioned dresser for a mug. Mesmerised, Keir fancied the material was like a living rippling sea over the sensual island of her body, and a surge of pure lust gripped him with a vengeance. The impact was dizzying, yet straight afterwards his head cleared almost miraculously, and he secretly marvelled at how just the mere sight of this woman could effect such a dramatic change in him.

Before Georgia had come to Glenteign he had

been angry and resentful at being forced to return to his family home, even though he'd always known that he would do his duty there. Mired in the past because of his surroundings, and the hurtful recollections triggered by his brother's unexpected death, most of Keir's attention had been consumed by his situation. But now—now he found his mind transfixed instead by the allure of this lovely woman...

Drawn by the pure rush of need that pulsed in his veins like one of the fast-flowing inlets that wound its way down through the Glens, Keir crossed the flagged kitchen floor to join her, walking up behind her without a word and sliding his arms around her waist.

'Good morning,' he greeted her softly, his voice deliberately lowered and his lips a mere half-inch from the tender place just behind her ear that smelled so divinely of her sweet erotic essence.

'I was just going to make some tea,' she said breezily, slipping from his arms as easily as though she were some silken will o' the wisp. 'Would you like some?'

Keir did not welcome the tumult of powerful rejection that kept his feet rooted to the floor. Her moving away from him like that was not the scenario he'd anticipated, and immediately his temper surfaced.

'You should know by now that I only drink coffee in the morning!' he snapped.

'My mistake,' she replied, unoffended and gave him a little half-smile. 'If you want to sit down at the table I'll make you some. Moira has already left to go grocery shopping in Dundee, so if you want breakfast I'll make that for you too.'

Regarding his stony expression, Georgia wished she hadn't been so hasty to free herself from his unexpected embrace. His hard, masculine body had felt so good pressed up close to hers, and his warm, enticing breath and the hypnotic blend of his aftershave had whispered seductively over her skin. But the truth was that she hadn't known how Keir would greet her this morning, after yesterday's events, and she'd steeled herself for the possibility that he might be a little bit cool with her.

After all, she had rejected his invitation to go back to bed, and with hindsight he might easily have concluded himself that it was better if they didn't sleep together again. Plus, he had made it quite apparent that what they had was merely something fleeting, and not something that heralded any right future for them both. Why else would he have told Georgia that the man she eventually ended up with would be lucky to have her?

'I don't want any breakfast. I'll just have some coffee.' Assessing her with an almost accusing glare, he seemed to suddenly and chillingly assume his role of somewhat distant employer, and Georgia's insides cramped in protest. 'You can bring it into the study when it's ready. I'll be in there working.'

'Keir?'

But he was already walking out through the door as Georgia called his name, and he did not bother to wait and hear what it was she had been going to say…

'The dinner party on Saturday night… Did you do a final count of all the acceptances and inform Moira how many were coming?'

Hating the deliberately formal tone he'd adhered to all morning—as if she were truly just someone who worked for him and had never been remotely anything else—Georgia briefly licked her lips before turning in her chair to reply.

His handsome face was unsmiling, yet no less compelling for the frown that creased his brow. Keir's annoyance was tangible.

'It's imperative that everything is right,' he interjected. 'Some of the "great and the good" from the local community are coming, and this is the first big dinner we've held at Glenteign since work on the gardens was completed. Apart from the curiosity and criticism that that in itself will provoke, you can be sure they'll be scrutinising everything in the house with a fine tooth comb… From the silver plate decorating the dining table to what kind of tissue paper we put in the bathrooms!'

'There's no need to worry. Everything's been arranged. I got up early to go over it all with Moira before she went into Dundee shopping this morning, and we'll do a final check again tomorrow.'

'And did you remember to tell her that the Dean likes his beef very rare?'

Georgia had already told him yesterday that she had. Now it was her turn to frown. She got the distinct feeling that he was spoiling for a fight. Was it solely because she hadn't been as warm as she could have been earlier, when he'd embraced her in the kitchen, or was it something else?

'I did. I told you—there's nothing to worry about.'

'I think I should be the judge of that!'

'What's the matter? Is your burn causing you pain? Why don't you let me take a look at it and change the dressing?'

On her feet before he could answer, Georgia walked straight over to his desk, despite his expression being less than welcoming and even seemed to be warning her off. A wave of deep unhappiness descended. She didn't want them to continue on for the rest of the day like this…like sworn enemies either side of a high wall. They had shared something wonderful yesterday…something Georgia would always remember. She hoped that Keir would too, after she'd left Glenteign.

'It's fine.' He held up his hand to indicate that she

stay where she was, his firm jaw clenched ominously tight. 'Why don't you just get back to work? I really don't need you to fuss over me!'

'Why are you being like this? I thought that—'

'You thought that because you let me seduce you, you should now be receiving some kind of special treatment?'

Georgia could hardly believe what she was hearing. Her cheeks burned with embarrassment and hurt. 'I thought nothing of the kind! And I didn't "let" you seduce me! It was entirely mutual…you know it was.'

Holding her gaze for long seconds, Keir finally turned his face away with a muttered expletive under his breath. 'Then why did you push me away earlier? As if my very touch burned you?' he demanded.

In the deep recesses of his mind Keir despised himself for allowing his acute sense of rejection to get the better of him. But when Georgia had not responded with the affection he'd desired, and had instead deliberately moved away, it had catapulted him right back to the centre of his childhood pain. Both his parents had been past masters at rejection.

Elise Strachan had been affectionate one minute and cold as ice the next, and when drunk had often pushed him and Robbie away. And if either of the boys had hurt themselves in any way, instead of comforting them, his father would admonish them with,

'You need to learn how to take a few hard knocks…stop snivelling and toughen up!' This from the age of three…

'Your touch did burn me, Keir… But not in the way you think.' Georgia's hand came down on his arm, and he sensed her heat radiate right through the linen sleeve of his shirt so that his whole body became instantly inflamed with desire.

'Then come here and kiss me!'

Suddenly Georgia found herself in Keir's lap, and he was holding her face captive as his mouth plundered hers. The wildly addictive taste of him made her writhe and yearn for him to touch her the way he had touched her in bed yesterday.

Just as his hand found her breast beneath her silky top and hungrily cupped it, the loud ringing tones of the telephone made them both spring apart.

'Stay right where you are.' Breathing hard, Keir scrubbed a rueful hand round his jaw before reaching for the receiver.

All the while he spoke to whoever was at the other end of the line his gaze cleaved to Georgia's with such riveting intent that her heartbeat refused to slow down, even though he was no longer kissing her or touching her. When he'd finished the call, his smile seemed to melt the very marrow in her bones as he lifted her hand to his lips to plant a kiss there.

'Now, where were we?' he teased. Glancing away, her mouth still tingling where he had ravished it only moments ago, Georgia suddenly turned ridiculously shy. Here she was, sitting in her boss's lap, letting him do the most delicious, delectable things to her with his eyes, his mouth and his touch, and she felt like the most gauche, inexperienced teenager. She might be a highly professional and competent secretary, a woman who had taken successful charge of her own and her brother's life from a very young age, but right now none of those attributes readily came to her aid…

Nobody had ever told her that falling in love could scramble your brain so much that when faced with the object of your desire it was impossible to even string two lucid thoughts together! Her glance fell almost with relief on the small metal figure of a soldier lying at the side of the blotter on the desk. She picked it up and examined it.

'Does he belong to you?' she asked lightly.

Georgia sensed Keir's body grow briefly rigid. When he didn't answer straight away, she wondered if she'd done something wrong.

'It belonged to my brother Robbie.' He took the miniature figure from between her fingers and sighed. 'It was one of a dozen. Robbie painted them all with painstaking care when he was about seven or eight…he spent hours and hours on them.'

'What happened to the others?'

'My father flung them into the fire in a temper, because Robbie hadn't been quick enough in bringing him his morning newspaper.'

'Oh, how cruel!'

Georgia's eyes had actually filled with tears, and Keir's lips twisted sardonically. 'You think that was cruel, do you? Well, James Strachan surpassed that particular act of spite many times, let me tell you! You wouldn't believe just what despicable depths the man could sink to when it came to the treatment of his family.'

Reaching across Georgia to get to his desk, Keir opened a drawer and dropped the figure of the soldier inside. Closing it again, he quickly fielded the pain and rage the memory inevitably engendered, and studied the ravishing girl in his lap with a blend of sorrow and regret. Even talking to her about the smallest part of his past he somehow felt that he was sullying her. This beautiful, innocent woman who had single-handedly raised her fourteen-year-old brother and sacrificed her own plans and dreams for love of her family…

That kind of pure, untainted love was a million miles from Keir's own experience. That was why he knew deep down in his soul that he couldn't expect their affair to go any further once the time came for her to leave. He wasn't the man for her…no. She deserved someone much more whole and psychologically intact than he was…

'I'm sorry that you and your brother had such an unhappy time when you were young, and I'm sorry your father was so cruel. I can't imagine what that must have been like. I only ever knew love and kindness from my own parents when they were alive. Was that why you told me not to judge a book by its cover when I first came here? Because this house doesn't hold happy memories for you even though it's so beautiful?'

She was regarding him with what Keir could only describe as infinite tenderness in her lovely green-gold gaze, and he couldn't deny the almost overwhelming wave of warmth that flooded his heart in response. Yet at the same time he knew it was dangerous to keep succumbing so easily to the compassion and caring that Georgia so naturally displayed. One day soon he would have to live in this house without her, and he'd better not encourage her to become more involved in his personal life than she was already. Ultimately it would be easier for them both if she didn't.

'I'm sorry…' He put a hand on her back and indicated she should get up. 'I really have a lot of work to do, and enticing as you are…I can't afford any more distractions today.'

To Georgia, Keir's words were akin to somebody

throwing a bucket of ice water down her back. Just when he had been opening up to her, sharing some of the pain of his past, he had all too suddenly closed down again and shut her out. Even though they had slept together. Was he subtly reminding her that she was after all only his secretary—and a temporary one at that? He was Laird—an important man in his community—and when he finally decided to settle down with a woman it would no doubt be with someone from his own class and background. The sooner Georgia accepted that and divested herself of any secret hopes she might entertain of becoming closer to Keir the better.

On her feet again, she crossed her arms in front of her chest and nodded towards the glimpse of white bandage beneath his sleeve. 'What about your dressing? I really think I should change it for you.'

'It can wait until later.'

'I only want you to be more comfortable.'

'I'm fine. Like I said…we have a lot to do, and the work won't get done by itself.'

Pursing her lips, Georgia turned regretfully away. 'Okay… But nobody can say I didn't try…'

The last thing she had expected was an invitation—though it was more akin to a command—to join Keir at the dinner party on Saturday evening.

For the past couple of days he had been kind

enough towards her, but there had been no more incidents like the one when he'd spontaneously pulled her onto his lap and kissed her, and—more pertinently—no late-night visits to her bedroom.

Georgia knew she wasn't imagining the distance he seemed to be deliberately putting between them. Telling herself that he must badly regret making love to her, she barely knew how she kept herself sane—but reverting to her usual saviour of hard work helped. And when she wasn't working alongside Keir in his study she helped Moira and the other staff in the kitchen, or ran errands for the household into Lochheel or Dundee.

She'd begun to understand that this dinner party was to be a bit of a 'statement' for the new Laird. Not only had he returned to Glenteign when he'd always vowed he wouldn't, but he'd also acted like a new broom—first getting the administrative side of the household up to scratch and inspiring new confidence in his staff, and secondly organising the bold new designs for the formal gardens.

Moira had told Georgia that the house had never looked as beautiful, and the younger woman believed her. Everywhere she looked polished surfaces gleamed, carpets and floors had been swept and vacuumed to within an inch of their lives, picture frames had been dusted, artefacts and ornaments fairly sparkled with the loving devotion they'd received, and the dining room and drawing room of a duke or a king could not have looked as decoratively elegant, she was convinced.

Georgia felt a bit like Cinderella learning that she was going to the ball. Now she'd realised how important this event was to Keir in terms of his reputation and standing in the community, she decided she couldn't let him down by borrowing the same dress she'd worn to the classical concert shortly after she'd arrived. So she went into Dundee early on Saturday afternoon and, after a frustrating two hours of not finding anything she particularly liked or could afford, found the most exquisite black cocktail dress in a small retro boutique down a cobblestoned side-street. She was delighted when it fitted as though it had been made for her.

When the time finally came for her to wear it, Georgia had spent a good half an hour beforehand in a scented bath, and had washed her dark chestnut hair until the little lights deep in the colour gleamed like tints of burnished copper. She took great care with her make-up too, and when there was nothing else to do other than drape her burgundy pashmina round her shoulders and take a final morale-boosting glance in the wardrobe mirror she left her bedroom to head down the long silent corridor to the staircase.

* * *

Keir was in the huge chequered hallway, greeting his guests as they arrived back at the house after being shown round the gardens by the head gardener Brian. There was a smartly attired member of his staff waiting beside him with glasses of champagne ready to place into their hands after Moira Guthrie had taken any unwanted coats and jackets to the downstairs cloakroom.

As if he'd been intimately attuned to the very moment she would appear at the top of the grand winding staircase Keir glanced round to see Georgia standing there. Everything inside him rejoiced at the sight of her. He had always considered her beautiful, but tonight in his opinion her loveliness excelled that of Venus herself. As he observed her one side of the Pashmina shawl slipped a little down one shoulder, and the smooth radiance of her perfect skin was inadvertently revealed in a black strapless dress—including the soft, sensual swell of her breasts. He hardly knew how he took his next breath he was so transfixed.

'Come and join us,' he invited, over an almost tinder-dry throat.

His gaze tracked every tread as she descended the staircase. When she reached his side, his blue eyes devoured her as though he would swallow her whole.

'You look stunning,' he told her, uncaring that the mingled guests drinking their champagne overheard him. Turning, he lifted a fluted glass full of the fizzing, sparkling wine from the waiting tray and placed it into her hands. 'Let me introduce you to my guests.' He smiled.

Georgia told herself she must be dreaming. But even amidst the spellbinding grandeur of the gleaming hallway, the champagne, and the interested glances of the other smartly dressed assembled guests, it was the man who stood beside her that held her attention above all else. His riveting features and commanding physique were captivating enough without the benefit of being dressed in the most exquisitely tailored tuxedo, so that he resembled the elegant hero of a bygone old-fashioned movie… Georgia's heart throbbed so hard she thought she might faint.

But Keir was leading her up to one person after another, and her dazzled brain was barely able to recall their names as they were introduced to her even in the very next second after they'd been voiced—because she was so enthralled by the man at her side…

'You'll be seated next to me,' he whispered in her ear, just after he'd suggested they all go in to dinner. And, with his hand thrillingly at her back, so that she felt the heat from his palm burning her through her clothes, Georgia just about managed to smile and nod her agreement.

CHAPTER TEN

CURIOUSLY, KEIR HAD not elaborated upon who she was to his guests, other than to say, 'Georgia.' And as the lavish dinner progressed, and the wine and the champagne flowed, she sensed the interest in her presence at his side gain momentum.

Finally, the elderly Colonel sitting to Keir's left, where he sat at the head of the table, leaned across and announced rather pompously over his wine saturated breath, 'You've done well for yourself, catching the eye of our young Laird, what? All seems a bit of a mystery, though, if you don't mind my saying. Where are you from? Who are your people? Do we know them?'

Everything inside Georgia froze. She knew that everyone at the table must have heard what the man had said, because suddenly other conversations around her seemed to die as abruptly as though a conductor had tapped his baton and ordered a silent pause. As she slowly let out her breath and the blood started to throb hotly again in her veins, she glanced across at the slightly piggy eyes examining her so relentlessly, as though she were some daring unwanted usurper at this dinner party. With all her dignity she said quietly, 'There's no mystery. I'm actually working for Keir—Laird Strachan. I'm from London, and my "people" are mostly gone, I'm afraid—but even if they were still living I doubt if you and they would have moved in the same circles.'

A hand slid over hers and gripped it tight. She almost jumped out of her skin until she realised it was Keir. He was looking directly at her inquisitor, and in the flickering candlelight there was something about the set of his jaw that told Georgia he was furious, even though his expression was outwardly benign.

'Colonel…I think your opinions are a little on the presumptuous side…if you don't mind *my* saying. Georgia is my guest this evening and I would have you respect both her feelings and mine by not interrogating her as though she were some kind of miscreant. As for your enquiry about her family—I can tell you personally that Georgia can claim parentage of the very highest caliber. I hope that satisfies.'

'Of course… Meant no offence. Do forgive.' Blustering, his cheeks momentarily as pink as the rare beef that the Dean of the Cathedral had just been served, the Colonel took hurried refuge in his generous glass of claret and the conversations around the table began to hum again, as though somebody had switched a radio back on.

Under cover of the other talk, Georgia turned her anxious gaze immediately to Keir.

'Perhaps I'd better go? My presence might be making it awkward for you and I know how important this dinner is for your reputation.'

'Don't run away.'

'I'm not! I'm just—'

'To hell with my reputation! If I can bear this, you can too.' He drew her hand onto his firm thigh, encased in its fine tailoring, and his heat instantly transferred itself to her body. It made her yearn to be alone with him, instead of having to endure this endless tension filled dinner with people she didn't like, and who were clearly judging her behind their falsely bright smiles. He was right…she *did* want to run away.

Her admiration for Keir increased tenfold, because he could endure such an ordeal and not show even by the merest glimmer of an impatient look or turn of phrase that he'd far rather be doing something else than wining and dining the local 'great and the good,' as he'd put it.

'Stay with me.' His voice lowered to a husky

command as he briefly and urgently roamed her candlelit features. 'I need you here…don't desert me.'

There had been no dilemma about whether he should spend the night with Georgia or not. In the end, Keir had simply had to admit that he had zero resistance as far as she was concerned, and part of him had thought to hell with the consequences. Increasingly throughout the dinner she'd been all he could think about.

Oh, he'd done his bit. He'd discussed the house, the gardens, the local politics in the community, and he'd smiled and been diplomatic. But after what the Colonel had said to Georgia Keir had made it very apparent that he would not tolerate any further speculation about either her person or her presence beside him at the table.

Thank God the event was over. His well-fed guests were now on their way back to their various homes, their effusive and complimentary remarks as they'd left, about the house and the gardens, still ringing in his ears.

And leave it to the Colonel to have the last word. 'Your father would have been proud of you, my boy!' he'd declared, as he'd unknowingly gripped Keir's wounded arm and all but made him cry out with the agony of it. The comment had elicited an ironic grimace on its own merit, though. Keir doubted very much if anything he'd achieved at Glenteign would have made James Strachan proud—but quite frankly he no longer cared whether he would have had his father's good opinion or not. The man was dead, and he was beginning to see that as far as the estate was concerned he could write his own history now that he was in charge.

Having told Georgia to go up to bed ahead of him, Keir now let himself into her room unannounced, and saw straight away that she stood in the golden light of just one small bedside lamp, wearing the same distracting short, silky robe she'd been wearing the night he'd returned from New York…the night of the storm. His heartbeat quickened at the curiously shy glance she gave him.

'It's got quite chilly tonight, don't you think?' she remarked.

'I've got something that will warm us up.' Keir held up the bottle of cognac he'd brought from the drawing room, along with two crystal-cut brandy glasses.

Approaching the bed, he placed the bottle and the glasses carefully down on the little oak cabinet beside it and pulled off his tie. The sound of the silk sliding against the stiff linen of his shirt collar was unwittingly sensuous to Georgia's ears. Knowing intimately what the impressively taut musculature beneath that expensive tailored shirt looked like, and remembering how his hard body had felt pressing down on her in bed, she knew she didn't have a cat's chance in hell of hiding the need that poured through her bloodstream right then.

Her cheeks burned so bright she must appear to him as though she had a fever.

'The food tonight was wonderful, wasn't it?' she chattered. 'And Moira did an incredible job of making everything look absolutely—'

'Here…drink some of this.'

A glass of darkly golden cognac was put in her hand, and Keir's long fingers briefly glanced against hers. Because she was so spellbound, Georgia lifted the glass to her lips and tasted some of its fiery contents without question. When the brandy's burn reached her stomach and ignited there, her whole body was infused with the most delectable melting heat.

'It's delicious.' Cupping the thick crystal tumbler between her hands, she glanced almost nervously at Keir.

After he'd whispered in her ear just as his guests were getting ready to leave that he intended to spend the night with her she'd hardly known how to get up from the table, because the sheer anticipation of his visit had rendered her limbs as weak as a lamb's. Now face to face with him in the softly lit bedroom, the gentle diffused lighting making his handsome features appear even more formidably compelling than ever, she knew she was utterly lost. Already, his gaze and his body—never mind his highly seductive voice—had made her incapable of refusing him anything. And she yearned to chase away some of the pain that she sometimes witnessed in his incredible blue eyes. Now that she knew some of the story of how that pain came to be there she craved that chance even more.

'What have you got on under that robe?' he asked her now, a dark eyebrow lifting ironically as he removed his jacket and then started to unbutton his shirt. 'If you want to make an already enslaved man even happier please tell me it's not very much…'

'I don't have anything on underneath.'

'Really?' With a slow, knowing smile, Keir moved towards her and took the glass of brandy out of her hand. Silently he placed it beside his own on the oak cabinet. When he turned back to Georgia he said huskily, 'Open your robe…I want to see.'

Seeing the shy hesitancy on her face, Keir took pity on her. 'Maybe this will help.' He bent and switched out the lamp, so that the only light left illuminating the room came from the silvery rays of the nearly full moon that filtered in through the open casement windows.

With the softest of sighs Georgia undid the belt on the flimsy little garment and stood there unmoving as Keir glimpsed the tender globes of her breasts and the smooth flat plane of her stomach. Gilded by moonlight, her long dark hair curled prettily against her shoulders. Any poet worth his salt would write sonnets to her.

'Any more instructions?' she joked, and he saw her shiver a little.

Again he smiled knowingly. 'Yes… Take off your robe completely and get into bed.'

As she did so, Keir turned to the swift removal of his own clothing. He had a delectable glimpse of Georgia's perfectly peach-shaped bottom bathed in moonlight before she quickly lifted the counterpane to slide underneath it, and he wanted her so badly that he practically hurt with the need. When he got into bed beside her, all her hesitation and self-consciousness seemed to vanish and she immediately welcomed him into her arms…just as if she was welcoming him home again. Having not experienced such an addictively seductive feeling in his entire life up until now—from any quarter—Keir was infused with an almost unbearable sense of rightness and a bone-deep pleasure.

Now, as his lips sought hers and he hungrily reacquainted himself with her extraordinarily sensuous taste, he sensed the oppressive weight of all his cares and darkness slip away as though by magic.

'Thank you for staying with me tonight…you made the whole thing bearable,' he breathed, gazing down at her rapt face. 'And I'm sorry you had to endure the Colonel's little outburst. The man was an old friend of my father's, and as you could probably tell he's still living somewhere in the Middle Ages as far as some of his views are concerned.'

'It's only natural that friends and associates expect you to be seeing someone from your own background, I suppose.' Her smile a little unsure, Georgia considered the man looking down at her with a sudden flicker of doubt in her hazel eyes.

'It's nobody else's business but my own!' Keir replied a little gruffly, hating the idea that she might think he was influenced in any way by other people's expectations of him.

'It's mine too, Keir. Don't forget that.'

'I would never take you for granted, Georgia…I promise. Now, where were we?'

When he would have captured her lips again, Georgia put her hand against his chest and stopped him. 'You were amazing tonight,' she whispered, her fingers playing lightly against the dark silky hairs coiling on his chest. 'The perfect host and the perfect Laird. Glenteign wouldn't be the same extraordinary place without you.'

'I never wanted to come back here again. I never thought I would…' His expression darkened a little.

'But you did, and everything's going to be all right, Keir. You do know that, don't you?'

'Is it? Somehow I can almost believe it when *you* tell me.'

Moving his hand downwards, he lightly stroked her breast, fiercely enjoying the soft gasp of pleasure that feathered over his already exquisitely aroused senses. As far as he was concerned the time for talking was ended...words were not what he craved at all. Forgetting everything but the lovely woman in front of him was what he wanted right now...that, and losing himself for a while...a long while...in the sheer enchantment of her.

Not for the first time in the few weeks since the dinner party did Georgia tell herself that this magical hiatus from real life that she was enjoying with Keir—working alongside him during the day and sharing his bed at night—would sooner or later have to come to an end.

He hadn't discussed the topic with her at all, and neither had either of them mentioned his permanent secretary Valerie's eventual return. It was clear that they were both keeping their own counsel about things—perhaps not wanting to risk spoiling what they had right now with worries about the future. But, even though he'd assured her that he wouldn't take her for granted, Georgia was afraid to ask Keir outright what his intentions were lest she sign her own warrant to heartbreak.

Autumn was upon them. There were signs everywhere, both on the estate and in the picturesque surrounding areas. She saw it each day in the rolling pastures and heather-clad mountains when she walked out early in the morning with Hamish. She saw it in the burnished leaves lying underfoot, and sensed it in the distinct nip in the air. Georgia also registered the changes coming in the magical dawn mists that covered everything in a blanket of icy ethereal silver.

It was a water-colourist's paradise, and some of the scenes she saw would stay in her mind and heart for ever, but not knowing what would happen, and almost dreading the prospect of going home again—even though she knew she had to—Georgia felt like a small sailing craft in the middle of a vast, unpredictable ocean, with nothing to protect her but God's grace from a possible storm at sea that would capsize her.

For the first time in her life she was in love. So in love that there was only one topic that never tired of recurring in her mind…Keir. She had never wanted anything in her life more than him. In the past all she'd wanted to do was provide a sense of security and happiness for Noah. She had hardly dared allow any personal wants or needs to come into the picture at all. Her deepest hopes and dreams had been put on hold for so long that she'd almost forgotten that she'd ever dreamed them. But now, with Keir, they had surfaced in glorious Technicolor to taunt her.

Leaning over the stunning old-fashioned claw-toothed bath in her bathroom one evening, Georgia trailed her fingertips in the steaming scented water. Satisfied that the temperature was just right, she went to the equally old-fashioned and beautiful gilt mirror there, and pinned up her tumbling chestnut hair in front of it before removing her light pink cotton sweater, then her lacy white bra. Folding the items over the white rattan chair next to her, she straightened again. Just as she did so, she experienced a wave of acutely hot tingling in the tips of her breasts. The sensation was almost painful.

Wincing in surprise, Georgia studied her body carefully in the reflection before her—as carefully as a scientist staring down a microscope at some fascinating sample on a slide. The dusky pink area around her nipples appeared significantly darker, and even with her own surprised gaze she could see that her breasts definitely looked a little larger. Cupping them, she felt a sharp stab of shock slice dizzyingly through her as she realised that they felt heavier too. Staring into the mirror as though transfixed, Georgia's clear hazel eyes easily registered the repercussions of shock that were ebbing through her.

'It can't be…can it?'

Moving to the rattan chair, she sank down into it, her arms crossed protectively across her chest as if to ward off even the possibility that she might be pregnant—because even with her lack of experience in these matters Georgia realised that that was her state. *But how could she be pregnant?*

Staring at the pink wall, with its tasteful cream border patterned with tiny pink roses just above the steaming bath, she made herself remember in detail all the times that she and Keir had made love. It wasn't difficult. There were days when she seemed to be able to think of little else. She wasn't on the pill—not yet—but he had always used protection…even when passion consumed them and threatened to make them reckless. Something must have happened that they'd somehow overlooked. Georgia had read that sometimes it could, even with the safest protection.

She shook her head with a groan. Why hadn't she paid better attention to her periods? They were always so regular, and the fact that she was at least eight days overdue should have told her that something was amiss. But her mind had been all over the place, and she hadn't even noticed. Now what was she going to do? She wasn't in a position to have a baby! Financially and practically, every which way, it wasn't a possibility. She had a home to run, bills to pay, Noah's business to support whenever she could. It just wasn't feasible that she could do all that and raise a child as well! If she attempted it she could potentially lose everything she had worked so hard to attain.

But, inevitably, the biggest question in Georgia's mind was Keir. What on earth was he going to say when she told him that she was pregnant with his baby? At this moment in time she didn't even know if he'd planned on seeing her again after she left Glenteign…let alone if he desired a proper committed relationship with her. Even the prospect of a relaxing scented bath to ease away the stresses and strains of the working day did nothing to release the tension inside her as she wondered just how she was going to break the news…

CHAPTER ELEVEN

GEORGIA DIDN'T FIND the opportunity to speak to Keir that evening, because after dinner he told her that he'd had an impromptu invitation from a friend to join him for drinks at his club in Dundee. Inevitably he would be back late, so she had tentatively suggested that it might be better if he slept in his own room that night and she in hers. Albeit reluctantly, Keir had agreed.

She'd made the suggestion less because of the fact that he might disturb her coming in late, and more because she'd convinced herself that it was probably wise to get some proper rest and sleep on things before broaching the subject. Her decision promoted the most disturbed night she'd had since coming to Glenteign—barring the night of the storm.

Nightmares of a baby crying and harsh voices telling it to be quiet, then a small boy curled up in the corner of an empty, dusty room, as if hiding from some lurking dark threat had sheened her body in icy perspiration when she'd woken, her face wet with tears, and she'd been struggling all morning to try and shake off the shroud of melancholy that inevitably lingered. And, as well as suffering the ravages of her nightmares, it was hard to think straight when the secret she carried had the potential to impact on her own and Keir's life so dramatically.

Georgia just had no clue how he would take the news at all. Now, watching him across the room from her desk as he put down the telephone receiver on his umpteenth call of the morning, she felt her heart slam almost sickeningly against her ribs as she decided that now was as good as any moment to break it to him. But still she hesitated. Eyeing him with a profound stab of longing, she concluded that he looked almost too beguiling for words, in a navy blue cable-knit sweater and black corduroy jeans, his slightly mussed dark hair reminding Georgia of a schoolboy who had rushed out of the door in the morning without remembering to comb it.

In her mind's eye she could see him as a young boy. With those amazing azure eyes of his and that perfect face, he must have been the most beautiful, adorable child. It was inconceivable that his father had ill treated him as he had. It was inconceivable to

Georgia that *any* adult could mistreat a child. Children were so precious…

The earnestly felt thought brought her anxiously back to her own astonishing news.

'Keir?'

'Hmm?'

'I was—'

'What?'

'I was wondering if you had an enjoyable evening last night, at your friend's club?'

Georgia grimaced at her own unhelpful diversion. Just where was her courage this morning?

Nonplussed, Keir glanced distractedly towards her. 'It was fine. Nothing remarkable.' But his expression had suddenly became more animated, as if recalling something of far more interest than whether or not he'd enjoyed the evening at his friend's club. 'I was going to show you some paintings—remember?' He was on his feet and opening the study door before Georgia could gather her wits and waylay him.

'Paintings?' She frowned.

'The illustrious Glenteign family legacy,' he mocked with an enigmatic smile. 'Let's get out of here before that bloody phone rings again!'

That day he showed her around rooms she'd never looked into before. There were so many of them—

anterooms and apartments full to the brim with paintings and priceless artefacts, all lovingly kept dusted and cleaned by Glenteign's devoted housekeeper and her staff. To Georgia, following Keir around like some enthusiastic and interested tourist, it was really like having access to your own personal museum.

'Look at this.'

He touched her elbow and diverted her attention from a regal-looking portrait of one of his many ancestors to the stunning gold harp leaning, against the door to yet another undiscovered room.

'Oh, how lovely!' Georgia declared, moving swiftly towards it. 'Did someone in your family play it?'

'No.'

He was smiling inscrutably, and she glanced up at him in confusion.

'Touch it,' he suggested.

As Georgia bent low to obey him, she realised it wasn't a real golden harp at all and she reached out to confirm it in amazement.

'It's what they call a "trompe-l'oeil." It's a painting…an illusion…of a three-dimensional object that looks completely real. As children, me and Robbie were fascinated by it.'

'It's amazing!'

As she straightened up to her full height again, Georgia saw the delight in Keir's face at her obvious pleasure in the illusion, and her heart swelled anew with love for him. Her feelings must have revealed themselves for a moment, because the next thing she knew he was pulling her into his arms and kissing her with a slow-burning hunger that made her toes curl.

When he finally withdrew his lips, she knew that her cheeks were surely glowing as pink as any chrysanthemum.

'What was that for?' she asked, her voice soft.

'Because I missed not being in bed with you last night. Would you have minded me coming in and waking you up?'

'I wish you had.' Her face troubled for a moment, Georgia let herself revel in the feelings of safety and protection that Keir's strong arms so tantalisingly engendered. 'I had a couple of really disturbing nightmares, and I couldn't go back to sleep after the second one.'

'Oh?' Now it was Keir's turn to look troubled. He brushed back some soft chestnut hair from her smooth forehead, his gentle touch eliciting a small explosion of delicious tingles up and down her spine. 'What were they about? Want to tell me?'

'No. I think it would upset me too much.'

And there was still the small matter of her pregnancy to discuss… Georgia sighed and started to free herself from his embrace. She walked across the elegantly varnished wooden floor to the other side of the room, pulling the opened sides of her soft grey cardigan together across her pink T-shirt and black skirt as if suddenly feeling the cold.

'I need to tell you something…'

'Sounds very serious!'

There was the ghost of a smile on his compelling mouth, and he shrugged his shoulders as if she might possibly be exaggerating just how serious the matter was. For an instant, Georgia wanted to delay telling him the news, and instead encourage this unusually happy mood he seemed to be in. But, as great as the temptation was, she knew she couldn't put her confession off any longer.

'It is serious, Keir. I think I'm pregnant.'

'What?'

The previously teasing light in his eyes seemed ominously to go out.

Georgia's hand subconsciously went to her stomach, as though to protect herself. 'I haven't done a test yet, but the signs are all there.'

'I'm sorry, but you'll have to give me a few moments here…' His hand absently touching the side of his temple, Keir appeared genuinely stunned. 'I always used protection,' he said, shaking his head slightly. 'How can that be?'

He doesn't believe me, Georgia thought, and for a long, interminable second she was sucked into a vortex of pure blind panic. Her own inexperience suddenly made her very afraid.

'I don't know.' Her hands curled into the material of her skirt and her mouth went dry as chalk. 'Perhaps we weren't always as careful as we might have been? Sometimes that can happen…' Her voice trailed off, and she hardly knew how she confronted the shock that clearly marked his handsome face.

'How long have you known?'

'I only found out yesterday… My—my breasts were tingling, and I suddenly realised that my period was over a week late. They're always so regular, and I should have noticed… But I—I haven't exactly been thinking straight these past few days.' Her glance was clearly distressed, and she pulled it away from the disbelief she was convinced she saw on his face, looking anywhere but at him.

'Well, clearly we have to address this—don't we?'

'Address it?' Georgia's knees began to feel weak. He sounded so cold…so unemotional…so detached. It was like a nightmare.

'We have to come to some decision about what we're going to do.'

Was he going to suggest a termination? Now she really did feel as though her legs wouldn't hold her upright. As shocking as the realisation that she was pregnant was, not to mention the glaring hard fact that her life was about to change beyond all recognition because of it, she knew she would never voluntarily travel down that particular road of anguish. She was certain, too, that when Noah found out he would not want that for her either.

'You're upset,' she said, her voice cracking a little as she looked up at him again. Her heart longed to bring back the seductive humour he had so captivated her with only a few short moments ago, but she thought that perhaps she would never be treated to such an event again. The assessingly clinical glance Keir gave her in return did nothing to reassure her.

'Upset? That's an understatement! How did you expect me to react, Georgia?'

'Well, how do you think *I* feel?' Georgia burst out, her eyes sparking with sudden fury. 'What do you imagine being pregnant means for me, Keir? I'm a single woman, supporting myself as well as helping my brother build up a business! How do you think a baby is going to affect my ability to earn a living? My God, you men can be so bloody selfish sometimes!'

Before he could answer her, Georgia ran to the other side of the room, pulled opened the door and rushed out.

The Strachan family portraits that gazed back at her from their gilt frames on the corridor walls seemed to mock her distress as she quickly passed them, as if to say, *Did you really think that someone like you could be part of this great family?*

In that moment Georgia was certain that she'd lost her ability to trust another human being for ever. She'd hardly known how Keir was going to react to her news, but she honestly hadn't expected him to act so coldly. It occurred to her that perhaps he thought she was trying to trap him somehow, because of his wealth and position, because of Glenteign. Maybe he thought she'd seen a chance to stop working so hard and live a far easier life? The thought was apt to make her want to lie down and die.

As she hurried, dazed, back down the grand staircase, Moira was coming up the other way. She carried a pile of folded laundry in her arms, and she didn't hold back on the warm, genuinely fond smile she bestowed on the younger woman.

'Hello, lassie! Where are you off to in such a hurry? Is everything all right?' She peered closer at Georgia's stricken preoccupied face.

'Yes…I'm fine.'

'Are you sure?' Moira's frown told Georgia she didn't believe her. Glancing round to check that Keir wasn't following her, and feeling secretly heartsick that he wasn't, Georgia sighed. 'I've got a bit of a headache, actually. I think I'll take a walk down to the beach and get some fresh air, try and clear it. I won't be long.'

'You do that, my dear, and take your time. When you get back I'll make you a lovely cup of tea. That'll soon help put everything to rights again.'

'Thanks, Moira…you're very kind.'

Although the temperature was a little warmer today, there was a distinct crispness in the air. Before she knew it Georgia would be home again. Keir's permanent secretary, Valerie, would be reinstalled at Glenteign, and everything would be just as it had been before Georgia had ever set eyes on the estate—or the charismatic man who owned it.

Inhaling a long, shaky breath, she started to walk down the almost deserted beach. Save for an elderly man, who watched his pet terrier dart in and out of the foaming sea, she had the wide sandy shoreline with its craggy rock formation to herself. Folding her arms across her grey cardigan, her long black skirt billowing about her ankles, she finally allowed the feelings she'd been desperately trying to keep at bay until she got there free rein.

All this time… All this time and she'd never known she could love a man as she loved Keir. She'd given herself to him because she loved him. Her virginity hadn't been such a burden that she would have given it to just any man she was attracted to. And now she was going to have his baby. By rights she should be feeling on top of the world. Except for Keir's hurtful reaction to the news of her pregnancy Georgia told herself she would be. But now she knew that despite their passionate connection, and her love for him, there was no future for them as far as he was concerned.

Probably one day, soon after she had gone, another woman—a woman from a similarly privileged background to his—would see his face next to hers when she woke in the morning in their bed. Another woman would come to know that sometimes he was haunted by his past, would learn to forgive him for his occasional black moods… And another woman would lie in his arms, her head against his chest, and feel loved and protected as she'd never felt loved and protected before…

Georgia pulled herself up short. But Keir didn't love her. That was the whole point. If he had cared for her in the slightest then he wouldn't have behaved like some aloof, distant stranger towards her when she'd told him she was carrying his baby. He would at least have reassured her that he would stand by her, come what may…wouldn't he?

She had no indication of who was behind her until the golden Labrador flew past her in a flurry of sand and wet fur. He stopped just ahead of where she stood, panting hard, his long tail wagging, his black eyes as bright and liquid as a seal's as he gazed happily up at her.

'Hamish!'

Immediately bending low to pet him, Georgia felt her heart lift at the sight of the animal, despite her sorrow. Turning her head, she looked up the beach, expecting to see Lucy or perhaps Euan jogging towards her. Both young people had taken quite a shine to the Labrador, and occasionally walked him for Georgia. But the tall, dark figure walking towards them wasn't either of Glenteign's younger staff members.

Georgia froze, convinced for a moment that her eyes must be deceiving her. Why was Keir walking Hamish? He'd never done it before. She didn't even know if he liked dogs!

She remembered when she'd first arrived his definite withdrawal when she'd suggested that the dog had sensed he was friendly.

Drawing near, he dropped his hands to his hips and blew out a breath. A gust of wind tousled the thick silky strands of his strong black hair and blew them across his indomitable brow. Georgia straightened and pushed her own windblown hair away from her face.

'When I was nine years old I had a Labrador very much like Hamish,' he started to tell her.

Transfixed, Georgia hardly dared breathe.

'I did something to displease my father… I can't even remember what it was now. Probably I just looked at him the wrong way. It didn't take much.'

He shrugged and glanced away from her for a moment, his blue eyes glittering.

'To punish me, he had the dog taken away. I never knew where he had gone and he wouldn't tell me. I loved that animal more than I cared for either of my parents...but, frankly, that wasn't hard to do. I think I've indicated already that they weren't the most affectionate people you could meet. Anyway, I vowed from that day on not to get too close to either another human being or an animal again. I'm afraid I even included poor Robbie in that vow...something that I've come to deeply regret. But then you came along, Georgia, and there was something about you that got to me straight away.'

For a moment his lips looked as though they duelled with a smile.

'You fascinated me right from the start. In fact I'd never reacted so strongly to a woman in all my life! It didn't take long for my feelings towards you to deepen into something even more compelling. How could they not when I learned of the sacrifices you had made for your brother? I was in total admiration. I'd never known anyone who'd acted so selflessly before...certainly I'd never known anyone who was capable of loving someone as much as you appeared to love Noah. When we first made love I was overwhelmed by the discovery that you were a virgin. And if I'm honest I wanted you to be mine right from that moment. I'm asking you now Georgia…will you be mine for ever?'

Her mind hungrily trying to absorb everything he'd told her, hardly daring to believe what he was asking her, Georgia trembled so hard she felt giddy. 'But what about the baby, Keir? You seemed so upset when I told you I was pregnant.'

'I admit I felt that I'd been hit by a hurricane at the news.' With a wry grin, he pushed his hands into his jeans pockets. 'But first of all I was cursing myself for not taking better care to protect you…and secondly I was totally overwhelmed at the idea of being a father. Having not had the best example of fatherhood myself, I naturally wondered if I was capable of being the kind of father I would want for our baby…can you understand that?'

Seeing her expression soften, Keir knew immediately that she did. Perhaps it was selfish and even arrogant of him to believe that she would forgive him for not immediately welcoming the news when she told him, but even so he didn't take Georgia's forgiveness for granted. She meant far too much to him ever to commit such a folly. Everything he had just confessed was true. She had turned his life around with the love she radiated so unselfishly, and Keir knew he would never be the same brooding, solitary, emotionally repressed individual again. She had even helped him to see Glenteign with new, far less jaundiced eyes. And now, with the advent of their baby, hopefully a whole new more joyful chapter would begin for the grand old house and its occupants…

'I do understand, Keir, and I already know that you'll be an incredible father. You've nothing to fear in that regard.' Tucking her windblown hair behind her ear, Georgia ventured a smile. 'But first I need to know that you really do want this baby, and that you won't feel that I've trapped you somehow.'

'Trapped me?' Taking a step towards her, Keir impelled her urgently into his arms and his gaze hungrily roved her upturned face. 'Sweetheart, you trapped me practically the moment I set eyes on you! I love you—and I only want the best for you. I want you to live life on your own terms, Georgia. I don't want you to put your own needs last on the list ever again—do you hear me?'

'I hear you.'

'Well that's settled, then.'

'What's settled?'

'We're going to be married.'

'We are?'

'If you think for one moment that I'm going to live in sin with you, then you'll have to think again! This family has certain standards to maintain, you know,' Keir teased.

'So you want me to marry you?'

There was a definite tremor in her voice, and

Georgia's heartfelt gaze clung to the riveting planes and angles of Keir's darkly handsome face as if she really couldn't bear to look anywhere else.

'Didn't I already say?'

'But you didn't even ask me properly! And you didn't ask me if I loved you either!'

For one horrendous moment, Keir was filled with doubt and dread. 'Well? *Do* you love me, Georgia?'

'Very much, Keir.'

Relief and desire shone from his glittering blue eyes with equal intensity. 'Then will you marry me, and make me even happier than I ever hoped or dreamed was possible?'

'Yes, my love…I think I will.'

Before he could say another word, Georgia threw her arms around his neck and eagerly raised her face towards his to receive his passionate, tender kiss…

Keir was indulging in another one of his very beguiling erotic fantasies. Only this time the shapely, hazel-eyed brunette who was inevitably the star of the show, wearing some flimsy, barely there scarlet lace concoction that he ached to peel from her body—preferably with his teeth—was only too real. And she had driven his desire to a whole new category of its own.

That seemed to go with the territory as far as his feelings for Georgia went, and since their marriage a week ago those feelings had intensified to practically fever pitch. In Paris for their honeymoon, they had scarcely left their luxurious hotel room, and Keir was beginning to wonder how they would ever describe the famous sights most people came to see to their friends on their return. But he really didn't care what anybody else thought. This woman, this kind, beautiful, radiant brunette, had turned his world upside down and he never wanted it put right again.

'Keir?'

'Yes, sweetheart?'

'I think I'm going to make you very happy.'

'You've already made me happier than I could say, my love. How you can possibly exceed that I can't guess.'

'Then you haven't got much of an imagination—that's all I can say! What about if I do this?'

Georgia peeled the flimsy scarlet panties she was wearing down her firm, slender thighs and took them off. Then she threw them over her shoulder and grinned wickedly. Keir groaned as she deliberately wriggled her bottom against his hips, and arranged herself to sit astride him on the deeply luxurious bed. Before he could utter a word, she bent and kissed him lazily and luxuriously on the mouth. Her lips tasted of wine, and the aromatic Italian coffee they'd enjoyed earlier and by the time she lifted her head and came up for air, with a sexy, seductive smile that would have stirred lustful feelings in a stone statue, Keir was so turned on that he physically hurt.

His pretty, virginal wife had discovered a real talent for seduction since they'd been sleeping together, and Keir had teased her about making up for lost time. Only he didn't want any other man to realise her entrancing new talent but him. And he planned on staying married to Georgia for ever…

'And how about if I do this?' She wriggled a little more, taunting his already burgeoning manhood with her warm, scented, moist flesh. His sanity already at stake, Keir locked his hands onto her slender arms and pulled her down towards him for a hard and voracious kiss of his own. As she sighed and moaned against his mouth he found her core, stroked his fingers inside and out, then positioned his sex at her entrance. Catching her lower lip between his teeth, he plunged deep inside her.

'And how do you like it when I do this, My Lady Glenteign?' he teased huskily, watching the gold and green flecks in her eyes turn into liquid heat as he thrust deeper, feeling her satin walls tightly enclose him.

'I like it…very…much…' Georgia replied breathlessly, her dark hair spilling over her shoulders and framing her enraptured face.

'Then you won't mind if we continue in this fashion for the rest of the evening?'

'I need to eat too!'

'Then I'll order strawberries and champagne from Room Service and feed them to you in bed. What do you say to that?'

'I say that you have some wonderfully inventive ideas for someone so—so steeped in tradition,' she panted, her breath coming quicker as her body convulsed above his.

Beneath her, about to surrender to his own passionate release, Keir was suffused with wave upon wave of unbelievable love for his beautiful new wife.

'That's because you inspire me, my darling… more…much more than I can ever tell you!'

It was strange returning to Glenteign as Keir's wife. But as they drew up outside the magnificent entrance and saw Moira with a few of the other staff, and Noah as well, all lined up to greet them, Georgia sensed that she would soon feel at home again. Every one of those people waiting to welcome them had an affectionate place in her heart. She'd grown close to them all in the weeks leading up to her marriage to Keir, so it wasn't as if she were returning to start a new life amongst strangers.

She had legally made the house in Hounslow over to Noah, and now it was his to do with as he willed. She'd even suggested to him that he sell it and put some of the proceeds towards his business. They had both moved on, and so had Keir. They had all left the past behind, and there was only an increasingly bright future to look forward to.

Now, after their intense two weeks in Paris, when she and Keir had shut out the world—for a little while at least—their thoughts had turned more and more to the coming baby. Whether boy or girl, they both knew that their child would have all the love, affection and support that Keir and his brother Robbie had so sadly lacked in their own childhood.

'You look absolutely ravishing, sis!' Noah caught her in one of his fierce brotherly hugs, and Georgia held onto him tightly for a moment before pulling back to look up into his endearingly handsome face. 'Do you think that the ugly duckling has turned into a swan, then?' she teased.

'Ugly duckling, my foot!' Noah shook his head. 'You were always beautiful, Georgia—but that's because you have such a beautiful heart. I'm just glad that you've found someone who appreciates you for all your assets!'

Turning round to catch her husband's eye, Georgia saw him smile at her unreservedly. She knew without a single shred of a doubt that Keir loved her more than she'd ever dreamed she could be loved by a man, and indeed appreciated every one of her 'assets'!

There was one more member of the household yet

to greet them, and as the big Labrador bounded round the corner from the direction of the recently redesigned gardens and made a beeline for the master of the house Georgia saw how delighted her husband was with Hamish's effusive greeting. He dropped down to his haunches to make a fuss of the family pet, and for a moment Georgia had a glimpse of the lonely little boy he had once been. Her heart all but leapt out of her chest with love for him.

'I told you he loves you!' she called out, laughing. Lifting his head, Keir grinned at her, and laughed right back…

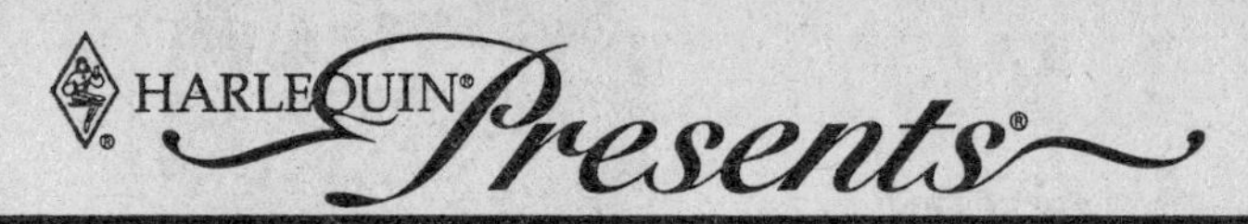

**The richest royal family in the world—
a family united by blood and passion,
torn apart by deceit and desire.**

By royal decree, Harlequin Presents is delighted to bring you *The Royal House of Niroli.* Step into the glamorous, enticing world of the Nirolian Royal Family. As the king ails, he must find an heir…each month an exciting new installment follows the epic search for the true Nirolian king. Eight heirs, eight romances, eight fantastic stories!

Be sure not to miss any of the passion!

Coming in August:

SURGEON PRINCE, ORDINARY WIFE

by Melanie Milburne

When brilliant surgeon Dr. Alex Hunter discovers he's the missing Prince of Niroli long thought dead, he is torn between duty and his passion for Amelia Vialli, who can never be his queen….

Coming in September:

BOUGHT BY THE BILLIONAIRE PRINCE

by Carol Marinelli

www.eHarlequin.com

HP12651

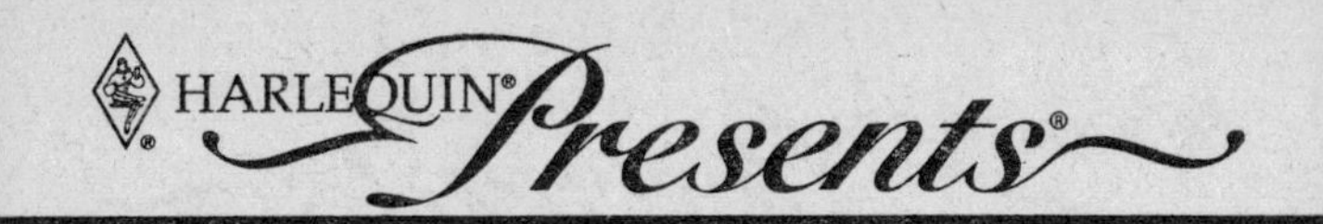

**He's proud, passionate, primal—
dare she surrender to the sheikh?**

Feel warm winds blowing through your hair and the hot desert sun on your skin as you are transported to exotic lands. As the temperature rises, let yourself be seduced by our sexy, irresistible sheikhs.

If you love our men of the desert, look for more stories in this enthralling miniseries coming soon!

Rosalie Winters doesn't engage in the games of flirtation that Sheikh Arik expects from women—but once Rosalie is under his command, she'll open up to receive the loving that only he can give her.

FOR THE SHEIKH'S PLEASURE

by Annie West